MW01407419

DECIDE & SURVIVE™

AGENT 355

Text copyright © 2024 by Ryan G. Van Cleave.
Illustration copyright © 2024 by Mike Anderson.

All rights reserved.

No portion of this book may be reproduced in any form without written permission from the publisher or author, except as permitted by U.S. copyright law.

Published by Milk & Cookies, an imprint of Bushel & Peck Books. Bushel & Peck Books is a family-run publishing house in Fresno, California, that believes in uplifting children with the highest standards of art, music, literature, and ideas. Find beautiful books for gifted young minds at www.bushelandpeckbooks.com.

Type set in LTC Kennerley Pro and Bobby Jones.
Graphic elements licensed from Shutterstock.com.

Bushel & Peck Books is dedicated to fighting illiteracy all over the world. For every book we sell, we donate one to a child in need—book for book. To nominate a school or an organization to receive free books, please visit www.bushelandpeckbooks.com.

LCCN: TK
ISBN: 978-1-63819-181-0

First Edition

Printed in the United States

1 3 5 7 9 10 8 6 4 2

CAN YOU WIN THE REVOLUTION?

RYAN G. VAN CLEAVE | MIKE ANDERSON

MILK + COOKIES

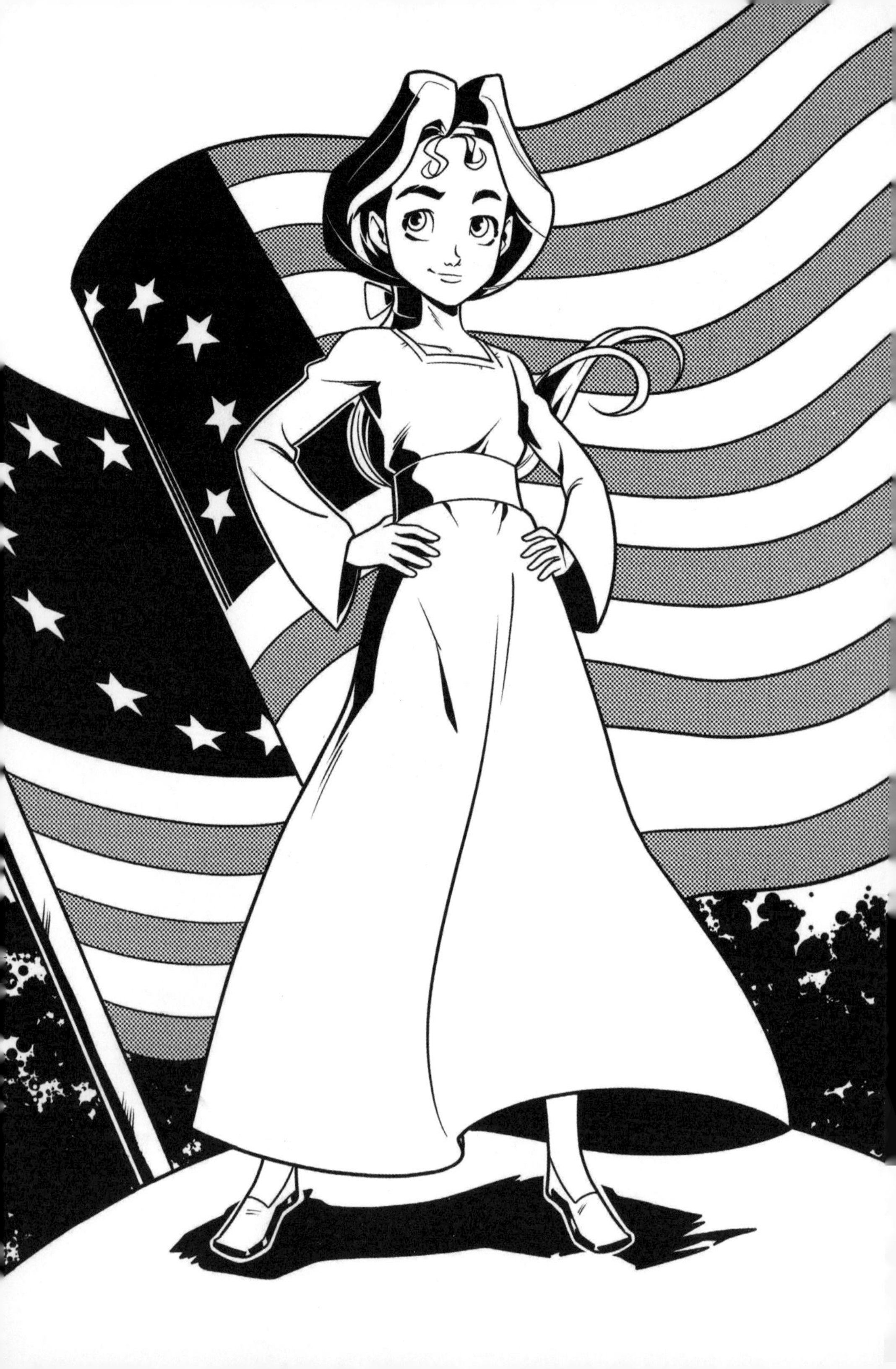

YOUR CALL TO ADVENTURE!

Dear Reader, this is *your* story. *You* control how history happens through the choices you make.

Don't read this book from the first page to the last. Instead, follow the directions at the bottom of each page. When you're offered options, choose wisely because your decision could end in disaster as easily as triumph.

No matter how your story ends, feel free to start over and create a different one with a new outcome.

Adventure, mystery, danger, and fortune await. Good luck!

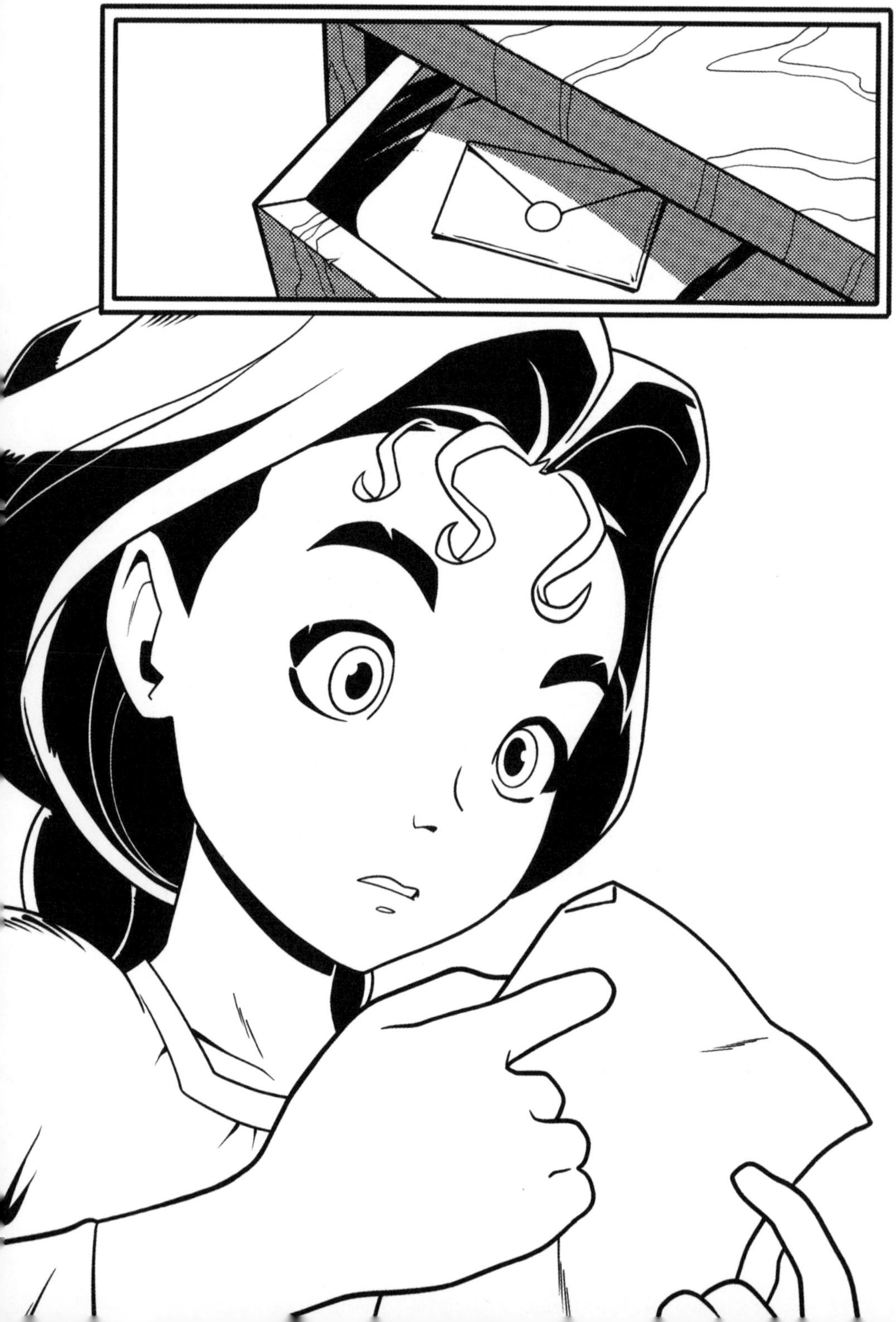

BACKSTORY

The Revolutionary War is raging between the Patriots in the American colonies and Great Britain. You don't think your parents are especially interested in politics or war—instead, they seem committed to keeping the family out of harm's way. Then a bout of typhoid runs through Long Island, New York, and claims both of their lives.

Death and disease are commonplace in 1777, but it doesn't make your situation hurt any less. You miss them dearly.

As you go through their belongings, you uncover a shocking series of documents written in your mother's elegant handwriting. You learn that your parents were diehard Patriots—people who believed British laws and taxes were unfair. They were willing to fight and die to break free of British rule.

As surprising as that is, you're stunned to learn that your mother was a member of the Culper Ring, a group of spies so secret that no one knows any of the others. Not even George Washington, the leader of the spy network.

Even though you have her codebook that's full of Culper secrets, you don't want any part of this . . .

until the afternoon when British soldiers drag off your best friend, Ethan, for making fun of King George III. As they take him to a prison barge, you decide to pick up where your mother left off. Since no one in the Culper Ring knows each other, who'll know that you're the new Agent 355?

Moving in with Myrtle Walker, your aunt, is the perfect way to launch your spying career and hopefully bring about an end to the war. She's a Loyalist, fully dedicated to the crown of England. Since she lives in the largest house in Setauket, New York, she's constantly surrounded by British officers, soldiers, officials, and other Loyalists. You've been around some of them before, and they all talk freely in front of you. They don't believe women understand politics, war, or freedom. Especially one as young as you.

They're wrong.

Life's about to get very complicated and incredibly dangerous, Agent 355, but that's part of what's so exciting. Are you ready to change the course of history and, perhaps, save America?

 **BEGIN YOUR ADVENTURE ON THE NEXT PAGE.**

YOUR ADVENTURE BEGINS

The party this evening at your Aunt Myrtle's mansion feels different. As you dance the quadrille with Trevor, the son of British Major-General William Tryon, it seems as if every pair of eyes is looking right at you. You spin and twirl to hide your growing sense of dread.

Does this gathering of soldiers in fancy red uniforms and their Loyalist friends know you just pledged your allegiance to George Washington and his secret group of spies, the Culper Ring? That you've committed to work against Great Britain?

When the dance is over, Trevor bows. "Thank you," you say as he selects an older, prettier girl for his next dance partner.

You take a deep breath, adjust your dress, and pick up the platter of sweetbreads to offer guests. Sure, there are servants to do that work, but Aunt Myrtle—your new guardian—believes eleven-year-old girls should earn their keep, too. "Life isn't free," she told you the day you moved in.

With her usual frown, Aunt Myrtle watches you

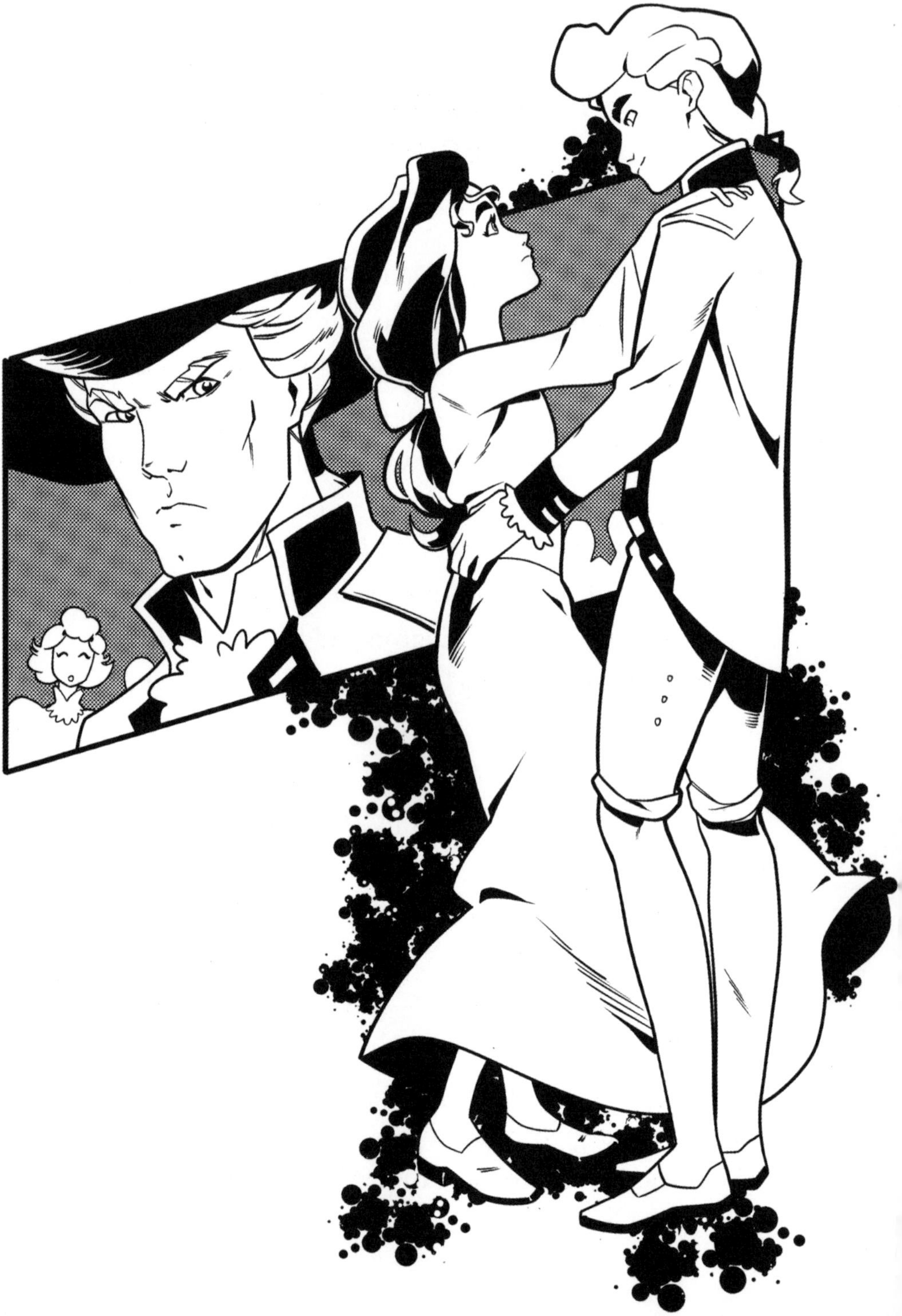

move through the crowd. No one else is paying any attention to you even as some grab sweetbread from your tray. It's almost as if you're invisible.

Snippets of so many conversations reach your ears. A problem with the buckwheat crop. A scuffle in the Setauket jail. A cousin preparing to propose to a girl from the city.

"I can do this," you tell yourself. "I CAN be a spy."

But you're not sure that's the case. Ethan was the brave one. But the thought of him starving on the deck of a grimy prison barge fills you with anger that gives you courage if not confidence.

A hand snatches your wrist. You're tall for your age, but the British lieutenant who has hold of you towers over you.

"Hold on now!" he says.

Your heart nearly stops. He KNOWS! You want to drop the tray and run. But where will you go? The British are everywhere. Long Island. New York. New Jersey.

 **TURN TO PAGE 52.**

"Hello, good sirs!" you say with an exaggerated curtsy in your threadbare wool skirt. "Would you be interested in buying turnips?"

Good thing you brought a snack with you—three raw turnips, each the size of a child's fist. So crisp and juicy!

"Be off with you!" snarls a lieutenant. The soldiers push their prisoners past you. It breaks your heart to see so many good people in chains like that, but what can you do? Delivering your message is the best way for you to fight the British and maybe get Ethan freed.

You wave as the troops vanish into the distance.

⮕ **TURN TO PAGE 102.**

"We're out of manacles," says a soldier.

The British commander's face sours. "I trust that you're better able to keep track of a GIRL than you are at keeping us properly supplied," he snarls at the man.

"Yes, SIR!"

"Then let's move on," says the commander. "I want to reach Fort Slongo this afternoon."

The group marches ahead. You follow.

It's your first real mission, and it couldn't be going more poorly. You promise yourself that no matter what, you'll hold back the tears. Spies don't cry, do they?

After an hour, a group of men appear from around the bend in the road up ahead. Soldiers in navy blue with tri-corner hats? Continental regulars! After startled shouting, they ready their weapons.

The British rush into a defensive formation. "Ready . . . aim . . . fire!" yells the British commander. Musket balls whiz like a swarm of hornets through the cloud of gunsmoke.

You crouch behind a tree as the Continentals volley back. Two British soldiers howl in pain and collapse. A supply barrel in a nearby wagon explodes from the barrage, too, sending wooden splinters everywhere. Salted meat spills to the ground.

It's strange that in such a wild, dangerous situation,

you notice how the meat in the grass—venison, you think—is almost a starburst pattern.

"Reload!" cries the British commander. Red-coated soldiers grab powder horns and refill muskets.

⮕ **TO FLEE WHILE THE BRITISH SOLDIERS ARE DISTRACTED, TURN TO PAGE 70.**

⮕ **TO WAIT TO BE RESCUED BY THE CONTINENTAL SOLDIERS, TURN TO PAGE 20.**

The trip to the cave took most of the day. When you arrive back at the house, Aunt Myrtle confronts you in the parlor.

"I've had enough of your shenanigans, young lady!" Aunt Myrtle yells.

"I was just—"

"Don't tell me because, Lord help me, I don't want to know," she says, shaking her head. "It's clear my fool of a brother didn't know a lick about raising a young lady."

Speaking ill of your father makes your cheeks burn hot, but Aunt Myrtle shushes you, insisting that with the help of the good Lord, she's going to make you a lady whether you like it or not. And the first step in doing so is taking you to her home in the city. "There's too much room out here in the country for you to find trouble," she says. "In New York, I'll be better able to keep my eye on you."

That doesn't sound good. But New York is big. Besides Philadelphia, New York is the biggest city in all the colonies. 25,000 people, you heard one soldier brag.

With that many people in one place, the opportunities for spying would be endless. Maybe spending time in New York won't be so bad after all?

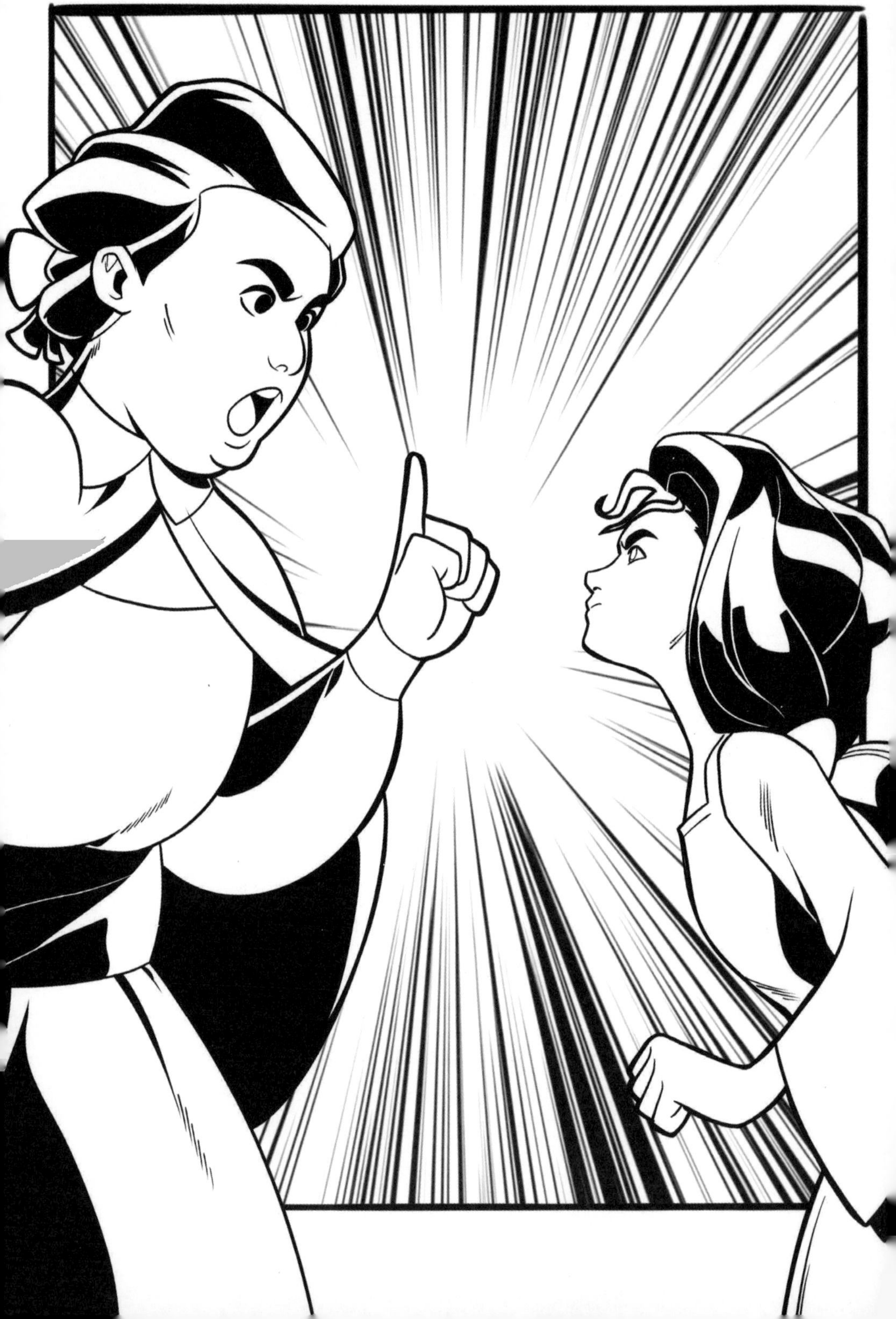

"We'll leave the day after tomorrow," Aunt Myrtle explains. "Now, go wash up so we can have dinner. It's baked salmon with mustard sauce—your favorite."

It's not your favorite, but the less she knows about the real you, the better.

"Sounds delightful," you say.

➲ **TURN TO PAGE 22.**

It doesn't take long—people remember when a customer spends money like he's a Livingston. Members of that powerful, wealthy family had mansions all over the city.

The cabinetmaker, Mr. Tully, recalls that same fisherman ordering two kitchen sets from his store. Mrs. Wennington the wigmaker sold him eight new wigs. Eight! She recalls the delivery address for those wigs being Gregory Muller's boarding house off Fletcher Street.

Something odd is happening. You can't let this go.

That night, under the cover of dark and dressed in your usual disguise as a servant girl, you creep up the back stairs of the Muller's boarding house. There are only four rooms for lodgers. Peeking through windows tells you which ones are taken by soldiers or Loyalist families, and which one is housing this money spender.

Is he home? You're not sure.

⊃ **TO BURST INTO THE ROOM AND ACCUSE THE MAN OF COUNTERFEITING, TURN TO PAGE 64.**

⊃ **TO SNEAK INSIDE AND SEARCH THE FISHERMAN'S ROOM, TURN TO PAGE 60.**

Ryan G. Van Cleave

➡ **TO SCREAM AND ACCUSE THE MAN OF IMPROPRIETY, TURN TO PAGE 36.**

The redcoats fire again on the Colonials, who return fire. A musket ball zings close enough for you to feel the rush of air on your cheek.

You knew being a spy would be dangerous, but this is ridiculous. What were you thinking?

"Don't just stand there like a stable post," yells a bearded prisoner who looks as if he hasn't eaten in a week. He pushes you into action. "Run!"

You yank up your woolen skirt and charge into the woods, away from the battle. A branch smacks you in the face and you trip twice, but you get up and keep going because your life—quite literally—depends on it.

The thundering cracks of musket fire eventually dwindle to nothing. It's just you and the quiet hush of the forest.

You still need to deliver your message and you're pretty sure you've got quite a few miles to go. Your stomach growls as you hurry down an old hunting trail, which allows you to pick up a bit of speed. The turnips you brought for a snack fell out during your escape, and the wild blueberry bushes have been nibbled clean by deer, squirrels, and bears, if the tracks are any indication.

With luck, you won't run into another British patrol.

You grit your teeth and continue toward the secret place where your mother's codebook said you could leave a message for a Culper courier.

➲ **TURN TO PAGE 102.**

Traveling westward on the North Shore Road is uneventful at the start. The trio of wagons and the half dozen servants move through the countryside dotted with farms and fields. You ride in one of the wagons for a bit, but the lousy road convinces you that walking is the far smoother option.

Partway between Setauket and the busyness of Huntington, one of the servants cries out. A half dozen men wait in the center of the road just ahead. They're a motley bunch, dressed in ragged clothes and armed with pistols and swords.

"Don't try anything foolish," yells one in a rough accent. "Just hand over your valuables and that's all we'll take."

The eyes of the most unkempt of the men run across each of the women in your group. He gazes too long at you before adding, "Maybe."

In all the time you've spent with Aunt Myrtle, you've never seen her scared. Until now.

She whispers, "What do we do?"

➲ **TO RUN OFF THOSE HIGHWAYMEN YOURSELF, TURN TO PAGE 75.**

➲ **TO TELL AUNT MYRTLE TO GIVE THEM WHATEVER THEY WANT, TURN TO PAGE 30.**

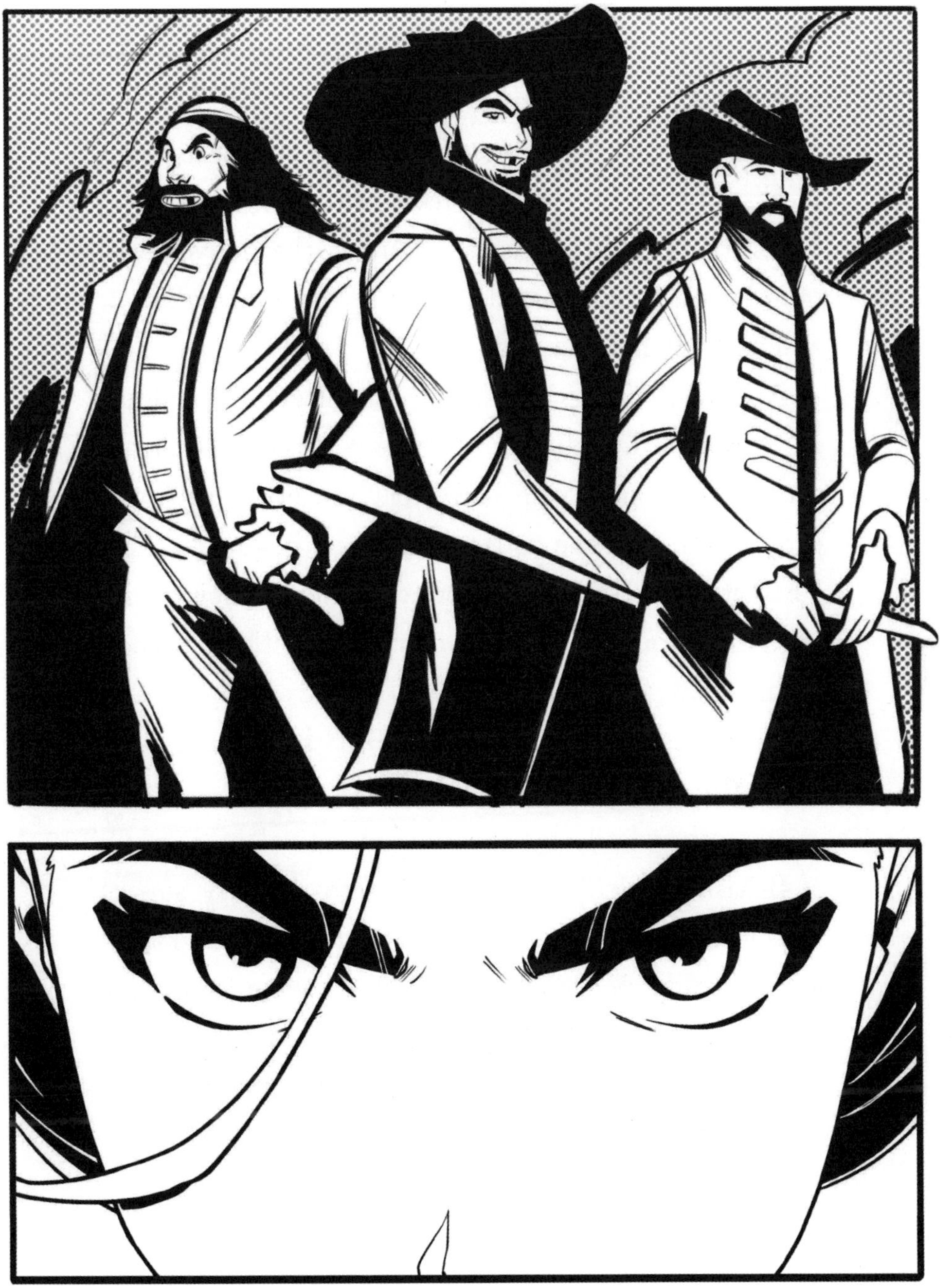

During an evening walk one evening, you sense that something's . . . different.

Rumors and whispers had been circulating for weeks, but it's not until a group of rebel sympathizers burst into the city square, shouting the news at the top of their lungs, that the truth seems undeniable.

The French are coming!

A crowd gathers quickly, a mix of curious onlookers, skeptical Loyalists, and fervent Patriots. At first, the news is met with disbelief. As more and more people gather in the square, the mood begins to shift. The Patriots continue to shout their news, their voices growing stronger and more confident with each passing moment. The crowd buzzes with excitement, and soon, chants of "Down with the British!" fill the air.

The already tense and uncertain moment becomes even more volatile by the sudden arrival of a group of British soldiers. They march into the city square in perfect formation, their boots striking the ground with a steady rhythm that echoes off the buildings. As they draw close, their leader, a stern-faced officer with a polished sword at his side, steps forward to address the crowd.

"Disperse now or there will be consequences."

➲ **TO JOIN THE GROWING PATRIOT MOB AGAINST THE BRITISH, TURN TO PAGE 86.**

➲ **TO HURRY HOME BECAUSE THIS ISN'T THE TIME TO FIGHT, TURN TO PAGE 101.**

As much as you love dressing up for parties, you're just as happy in a long wool skirt and a plain headscarf or bonnet. Your parents weren't especially wealthy, so wearing homespun clothes reminds you of those simpler, happier days.

But you're a spy now, and simple clothes are now a tool to help you do your job. With a few adjustments, you look just like a young maid. It's a fairly believable disguise!

While Aunt Myrtle oversees repairs on the stable, you grab a flask of cider, some turnips, and a small knife. You'll be lucky to get to your destination before noon unless you borrow a horse. Aunt Myrtle doesn't mind you running off on your own—she doesn't pay much attention to you, honestly—but she doesn't think it's appropriate for a young lady to ride a horse. Since she was down at the stables, there was no way to get a horse without her noticing.

The last thing you needed was for her to start talking again about sending you to Mrs. Langley down the way who taught so many of the other girls sewing and embroidery. Or insisting you shadow her all day so you could learn how to properly manage a household.

So, you walk.

The main roads aren't safe because the British are

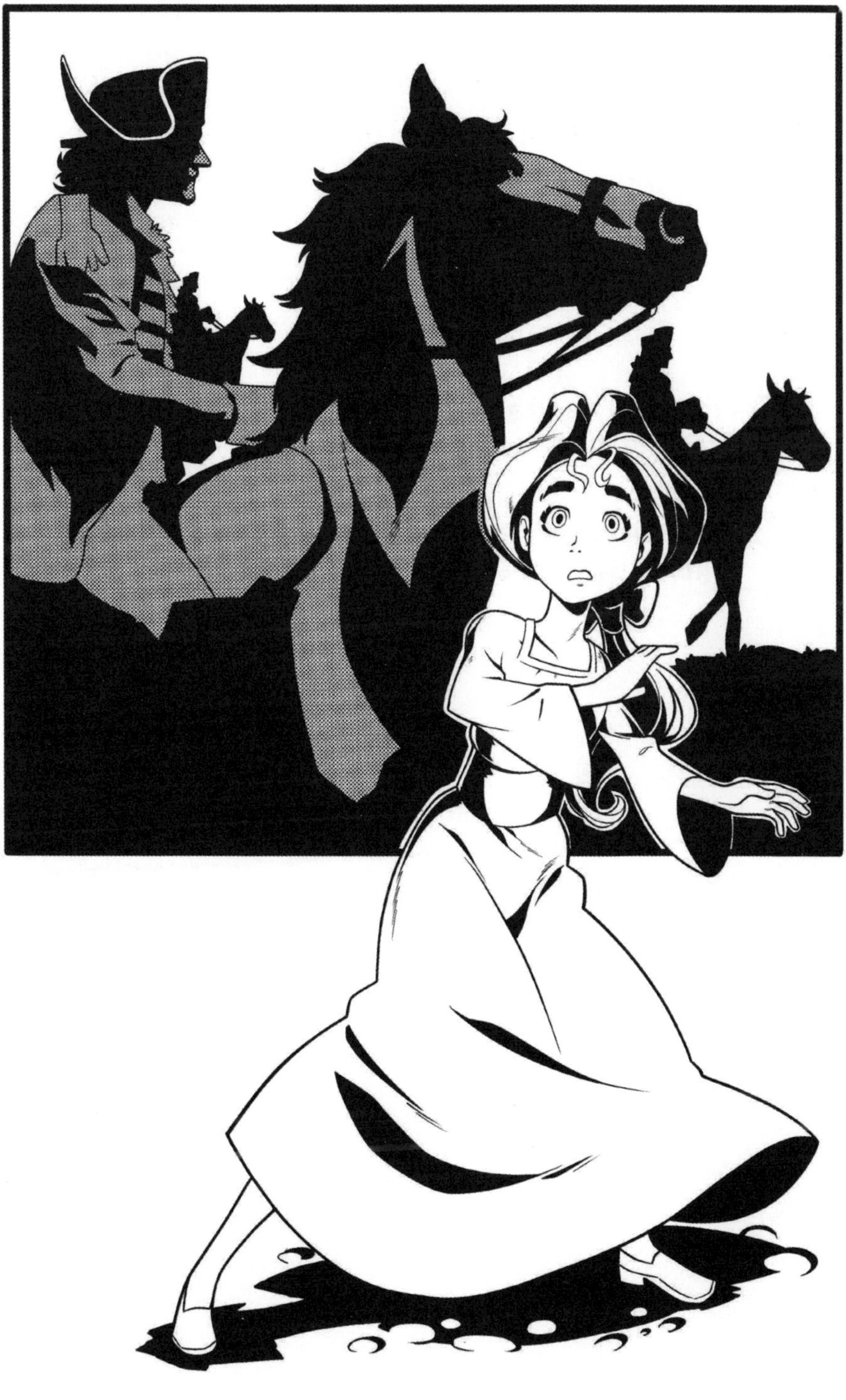

everywhere, so you stick to back roads as best you can. But sometimes there's no good option. You have to take the main pathways.

On the road ahead—the clop of hooves! It's British dragoons herding anti-British rebels and suspected spies to a prison ship.

⮕ **TO HIDE BEHIND BUSHES AND WAIT FOR THEM TO PASS, TURN TO PAGE 66.**

⮕ **TO STEP BOLDLY ONTO THE ROAD AND TRY TO FOOL THEM, TURN TO PAGE 12.**

You carefully write your message between the lines of a pro-British pamphlet. The Culper Ring's invisible ink works well, but the milky lime juice reeks until it dries.

Once you enter the busy street, you feel the eyes of British soldiers and Loyalist citizens on you. Do they know? Do they suspect?

You keep your breathing slow and steady as you enter the office of a shipping company that your Culper Ring codebook says can be used to send messages. You drop the pamphlet into a crate earmarked for delivery to a church in Suffolk County. From there, it'll be passed all the way up to General Washington himself.

"May I help you, miss?" asks the shipping clerk when he finishes with another customer. He scratches at his salt-and-pepper chin stubble while he waits for your answer.

"Nothing for now," you say, relieved to have the message out of your hands. "Thank you!"

You head home, feeling a hundred pounds lighter. Spy work—and being on your guard all the time—is exhausting.

 **TURN TO PAGE 31.**

"Take what you want," you say, as much to Aunt Myrtle as to the robbers. "We won't cause any trouble."

The leader dismounts and walks toward you, his features mostly obscured by the shadow of a wide-brimmed hat. He's wearing a long coat made of rough leather that's seen better days.

"What's in the trunk?" he growls.

Aunt Myrtle's footman, Benjamin, hands over the silver inlaid trunk holding Aunty Myrtle's toiletries. Not fast enough, apparently.

The robber clobbers Benjamin with the butt of his pistol. Among all of the servants, Benjamin is the closest to you in age. Plus, he's always been sweet to you.

"Hey!" you say, but a ferocious look from the robber makes you fall silent. As much as you hate standing by, spies aren't soldiers—they work in the shadows. You try to memorize this man's face so you might one day get your revenge.

"What are you looking at, blue eyes?" he says. He reaches out a grubby hand to touch your face. You recoil, which makes his face twist into a scowl.

"Why I'll—"

You never learn the rest of that threat because a heavily armed British patrol has arrived to save the day.

➲ **TURN TO PAGE 84.**

Three nights later, you discover a coded message tucked inside your freshly laundered nightclothes atop your dresser. You ask Benjamin and the other servants if anyone had been in your second-floor bedroom, but no one has seen anything.

"Is anything wrong?" Benjamin asks. He's always keeping an eye out for you. What a sweetie.

"No, thanks," you tell him. "I just thought . . . nothing. Thanks."

Back in your room, you shut the door and examine the message. The code is one used by the Culper Ring, so at least you know who sent it. And, of course, they're able to sneak into your room and leave behind a note without anyone noticing. That's just one of the many things that spies do.

Still . . . what might be so important that they reached out to you like this for the first time?

By candlelight, you translate the message with your codebook.

Washington wants you to spread word of a fake Continental army attack on New York City! He hopes General Clinton will keep the British troops in the city instead of attacking the French soldiers when they arrive.

It's up to you, Agent 355.

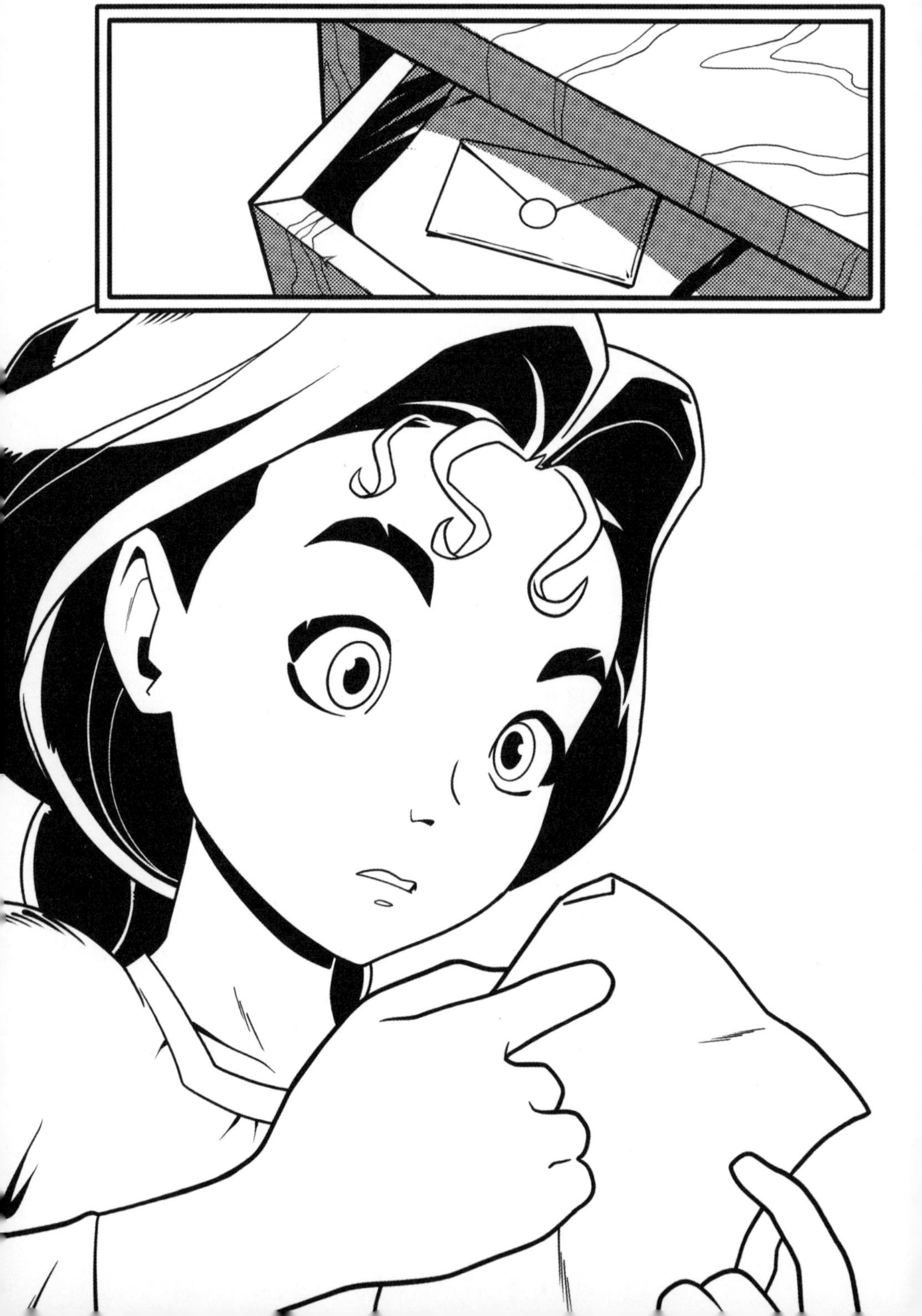

Most evenings, Benjamin goes to a nearby tavern to play whist or piquet with servants from other families.

➲ **TO ENLIST HIS HELP IN SPREADING THIS NEWS, TURN TO PAGE 100.**

➲ **TO CREATE A FALSE MILITARY DOCUMENT, TURN TO PAGE 56.**

➲ **TO GOSSIP WIDELY ABOUT WASHINGTON'S "ATTACK" ON NEW YORK CITY, TURN TO PAGE 38.**

Some spies are as good as thieves at picking pockets. Not you. So, instead of slipping your hand into a British soldier's pocket, you stroll by the stack of lumber that just came off a wagon. The smell of fresh-cut pine is thick in the air.

You can't just drop your document anywhere. It must be discovered somewhere believable.

That's when you notice a stump in the weeds behind the building. You head over and sit on it, pretending to adjust your shoe. The document is in hand, ready to slide into one of the insect-chewed hollows.

Your heart skips a beat when a worker comes to your side.

"Need assistance, my lady?" he asks. He's a Loyalist. All of them are. Worse, eight redcoats mill about, overseeing the operation.

You adjust so your linen skirt covers your hand and the forged document.

"Is the captain signaling?" you ask, pointing to a soldier with a sword. The officers almost always have swords, while the regular soldiers have muskets with bayonets.

The man turns. You stuff the papers into the stump hollow just far enough to hide it but not so far as for it to go undetected if anyone walks close by. Then you get up and dust yourself off.

He says, "That's not my captain. That's the supply clerk."

"Oh," you say, though of course you know that higher-level supply clerks often wear swords, as do officers. "My mistake. Uniforms all look the same to me, I'm afraid."

He seems fooled by your words.

➲ **TURN TO PAGE 69.**

You can hear the man inside his room. He's got a deep, rattling way of breathing, and there's the constant shuffle of papers, too. Peering through the keyhole, you think you see stacks of money. Mountains of it.

The best way to bring in help is to scream, so you cup your hands and shriek like a barn owl. Everyone comes running at the sound, including Mr. Muller and a British soldier from one of the other rented rooms.

"What's this?" Mr. Muller asks. The sleepy-looking soldier in the nightcap and cotton breeches holds a pistol at the ready.

You accuse the counterfeiter of behaving inappropriately with you. The British might be invaders, but they have a strong sense of propriety. The man shares documents with Mr. Muller and the soldier, proving that he's some kind of high-level British operative. Those papers give him all the authority in the world.

Uh oh.

"That girl is a liar," the man says, leveling a finger at you.

As you're hauled off to prison, you wonder if you might've made a better choice. After all, screaming for help and falsely accusing someone of misdoings isn't all that spy-like, and it's not very nice either.

THE END

"Did you hear?" you whisper at every inn, alehouse, and general store. "George Washington's going to free New York!"

"How do you know?" the haberdasher asks. As always, he's wearing the latest in men's fashion that he sells in his shop. His blue woolen beret is as fancy as his silk stockings with clockwork embroidery.

"My cousin's a lieutenant in the Continental Army," you explain.

You repeat variations of that story to traders, street vendors, and theater performers. Anytime British soldiers aren't around, you tell your wild tale.

People love gossip, and before long, word of Washington's impending attack is alive in the streets of New York City. Everyone from tavern owners to tinsmiths to watchmakers to coopers to messenger boys is talking about it.

Great job, Agent 355!

➲ **TURN TO PAGE 69.**

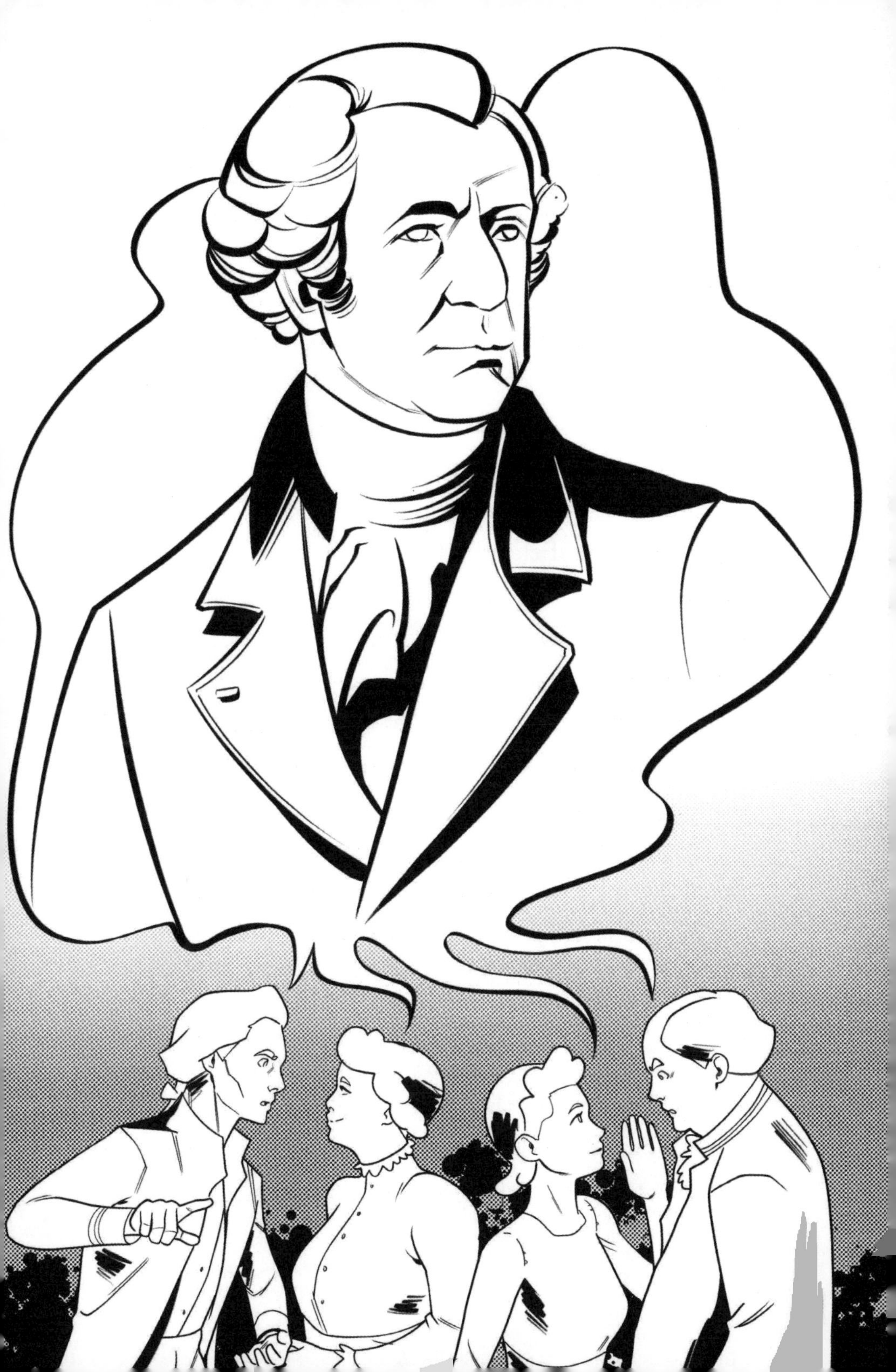

To do a job right means to take your time, and that's what you do. You owe it to the Culper Ring to get answers.

You check every drawer. You look under the bed. You examine the unconscious man's pockets.

Finally, you've collected everything that interests you as a spy: a sample of the money, a ledger, and a note written in a strange code.

You douse the room's light and slip back out the way you came. Beneath the cold glare of moonlight, you stroll past businesses whose windows are shuttered and dark. The sound of your footsteps echoes off the buildings, creating an eerie and lonely atmosphere. The only other sounds are the occasional barking dog or the distant creaking of a wagon as it winds its way through the city.

The streets are mostly deserted save for the occasional late-night walker or a night watchman. You avoid the most unsavory parts of New York City, catching glimpses of brothels and taverns as you hurry toward home.

When you arrive, you arrange the stack of empty molasses barrels on the side of the house so you can reach your second-story bedroom window, taking care not to make any noise. Thankfully, the cooper's apprentices haven't come to recycle the barrels yet or you'd have a very hard time getting back to your room without the rest of the household noticing.

➲ **TURN TO PAGE 79.**

Aunt Myrtle is beaming when she receives an invitation to the Christmas party being thrown at the house of Major John André because he's smart, charming, and politically powerful. You're equally happy to be allowed to tag along because he's the head of British intelligence operations in New York.

Plus, it's been forever since you've had an excuse to wear your pink silk taffeta gown with puffed sleeves and a fitted bodice.

You mingle and smile and sip spiced cider as Aunt Myrtle works her way through the crowded house, making sure to speak with everyone there. She's a gossip and a social climber. This is the party of her dreams.

The house is quite pretty, lit bright by candlelight and featuring plenty of wreaths, garlands, and festive greenery. It's the sort of affair that'd take servants an entire day to set up, and that doesn't account for the food. Fruits tarts, macarons, and cream puffs. A cracker plate with cheddar, Parmesan, and Roquefort. Oysters, clams, and lobster.

The roasted pheasant in raspberry sauce smells so good that you can't help yourself. You have a taste while you move through the crowd, watching, listening, learning.

That's when you notice your host, Major John

André, having a hushed conversation in a shadowy corner of his study.

You mingle closer. Who is the major scheming with?

You recognize her from Aunt Myrtle's parties. It's Peggy Shippen, a Philadelphia socialite who is sympathetic to the British.

And her husband, Benedict Arnold—a fiery-tempered officer in the Continental army.

➲ **TO SNEAK CLOSER AND TRY TO HEAR THEIR PLANS, TURN TO PAGE 105.**

➲ **TO WAIT FOR A BETTER CHANCE TO SPY ON THEM LATER, TURN TO PAGE 98.**

"What are you doing there, mum?" asks one of the British soldiers that seemingly appeared out of nowhere.

They're a dozen paces away. Hopefully, just far enough to miss the quiet *plunk* of your sack of tools being kicked into the water. It's bad enough you're holding onto the rope of a boat you were moments away from stealing. To have a crowbar, hammer, and wire cutters, too?

"I'm just resecuring my auntie's boat," you say with all the conviction you can muster. "I was out for a stroll, and I noticed it'd come loose from its mooring."

"And the water?" one asks.

"Huh?" you say.

His eyes narrow. "You're soaking wet. How's that the case if you're just retying a boat?"

"Clumsy me. I fell in!"

They don't believe you, but you weave a compelling story about how it all allegedly happened. Eventually they let you go since they have no real evidence of your wrongdoing, but they promise they'll be keeping an eye on you from now on because there's no room for rebels, traitors, thieves, or troublemakers in New York City.

They're not kidding. From that day on, anywhere

you go, you see the eyes of soldiers and Loyalists on you.

There's no way for you to engage in spycraft now. With so many British soldiers paying attention to your every move, you're just a civilian who must let others make the choices that affect history.

THE END

"I won't do it. I won't betray America," you say.

Your blood runs cold when Benedict Arnold drains the last of his brandy before saying, "Then I can't let you leave."

He puts his fingers to his mouth and lets out a shrill whistle. Redcoats burst from the shadows where they'd clearly been waiting, listening to the entire conversation. How did you miss them? How did you not realize you've been under the watchful eyes of the British for months?

You struggle and squirm as soldiers grab your arms. Escape isn't an option. Maybe it never was.

Aunt Myrtle comes outside because of the commotion, but her pleadings don't sway Benedict Arnold or Major André, who tell the soldiers to take you away. Perhaps they'll take you to the same prison ship that serves as Ethan's home. It'd be nice to see him one last time.

THE END

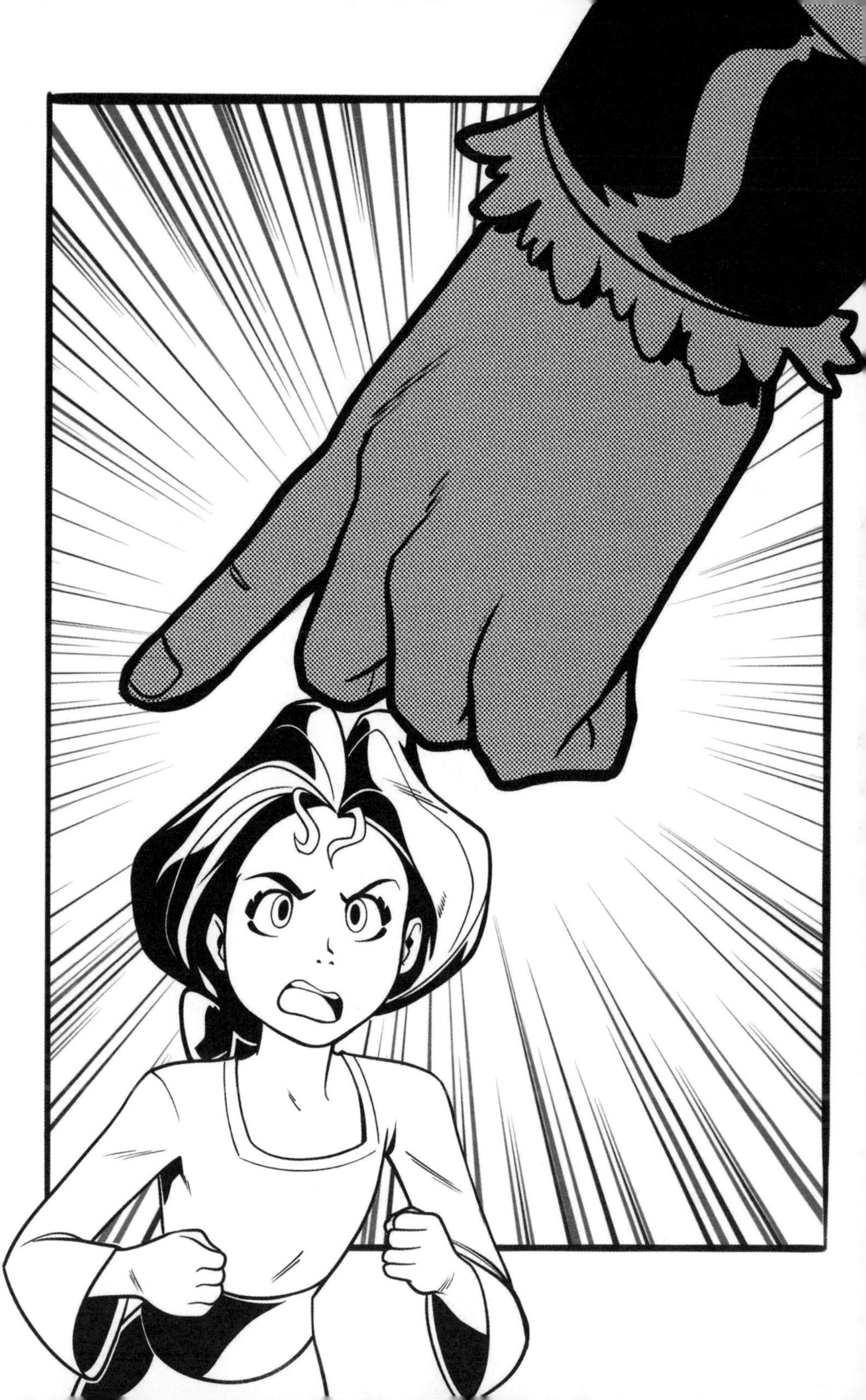

It's been years since you've been to the city. The towering walls and fortifications ringing the perimeter are new—a constant reminder of the city's importance as a strategic stronghold. Your group passes through checkpoints and is subjected to questions and scrutiny by guards looking for signs of rebellion or subversion. With Aunt Myrtle by your side, it's still a daunting task to reach your destination.

You're struck by the sheer size and complexity of New York. The buildings themselves are a strange mix of old and new, with grand mansions and elegant shops standing alongside dilapidated houses and run-down taverns. In some places, huge brick buildings rise on either side of the street, with bustling crowds of people, wagons, and horse-drawn carriages moving in every direction. Chimneys spew dark curls of smoke into the air. The sound of hooves and the clang of metal echo through the streets, even at this late hour.

The atmosphere is tense and anxious. This isn't a safe place for anyone, let alone someone with secrets like you.

Be careful, Agent 355.

➲ **TURN TO PAGE 72.**

The letter reveals that General Clinton is preparing a massive attack on the tip of Long Island . . . right where French transport ships are supposed to land in merely a week.

An army of redcoats and nine British warships are roaring toward New York right now!

Leaving a message for a Culper courier in the cave will take too long. You need something faster. What options does your mother's codebook give you for getting a fast message to the Culper Ring?

⇨ **TO SEND A WARNING TO THE CULPER RING USING INVISIBLE INK, TURN TO PAGE 29.**

⇨ **TO PUT A CODED MESSAGE IN A NEWSPAPER ARTICLE, TURN TO PAGE 104.**

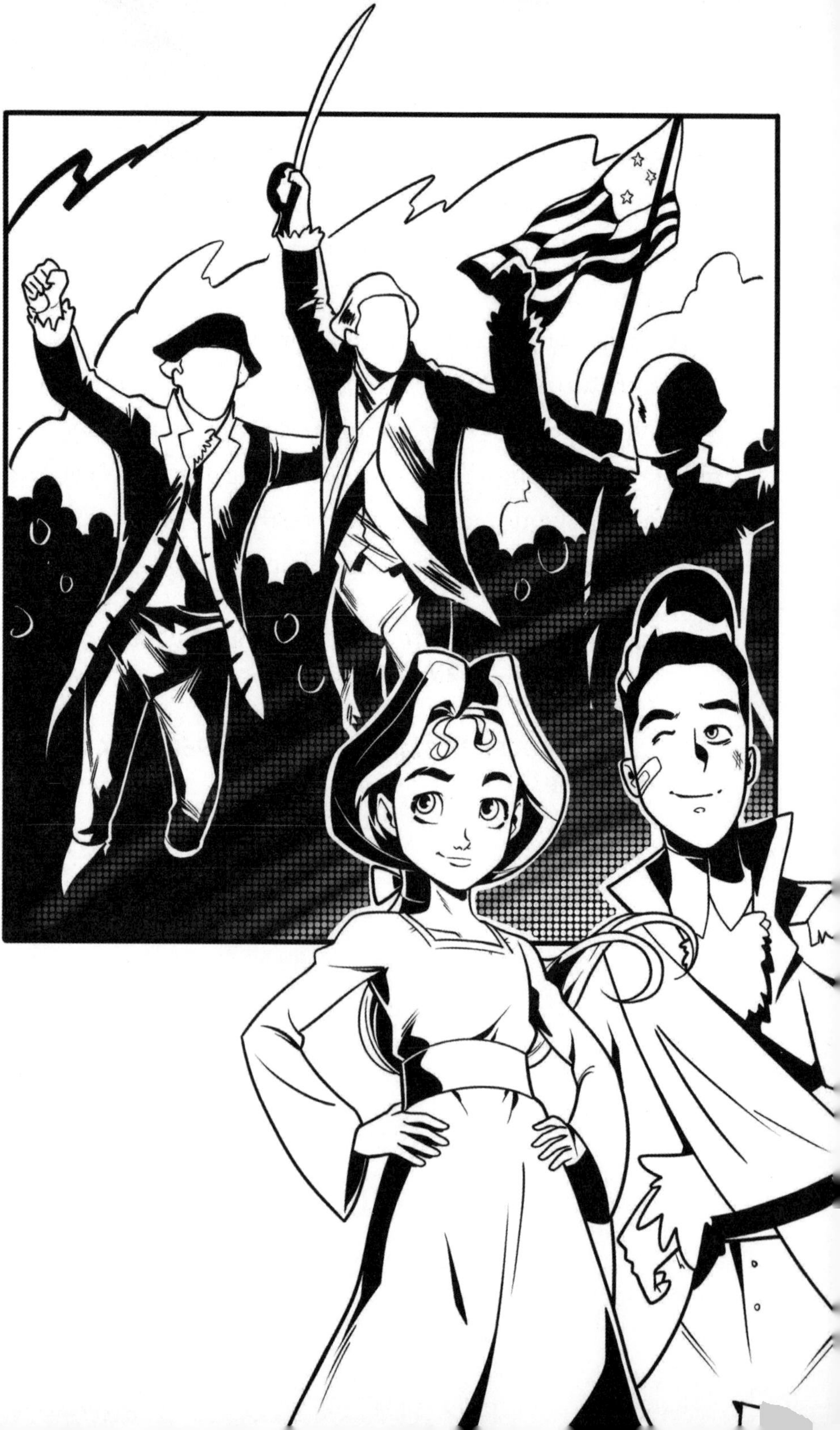

Sometimes a spy must get extremely creative to get the job done, and by finding this hidden page, you've done exactly that!

Through the power of unexpected choices, admirable courage, and incredible luck, you sneak onto the HMS *Scorpion*—the prison ship in Wallabout Bay—and rescue your best friend, Ethan. Together, the two of you rally the Colonials into an anti-British mob that drives every one of those British intruders straight out of the colonies for good.

You've saved the day, Agent 355. America owes you a huge debt of gratitude.

Not bad for taking a little chance, right?

THE END

The soldier's face breaks into a smile. "I remember you from the picnic last month. You're Myrtle Henderson's niece, aren't you?"

You nod. Since typhoid claimed the lives of your parents a few months back, it's just been you and Aunt Myrtle, the woman you don't dare trust.

He takes two pieces of sweetbread and asks where the champagne is. You point, your hand shaking.

"Thank you," he says with a small bow. With his free hand, he smooths out the front of his high-collared coat and adjusts the black cravat around his neck.

Even after he disappears into the crowd, your heartbeat thunders. All you can think about are prison ships, whippings, and hangings. Plus, the incriminating Culper Ring codebook tucked beneath your mattress upstairs.

Have you made a terrible mistake?

Just last week, a Loyalist was beaten to death in front of the bakery shop. You had walked past just as the body was loaded into the cart.

Some people are cut out to be spies, and some aren't.

Are you?

➲ **TO GIVE UP ON THE DANGEROUS FOOLISHNESS OF BEING A SPY AND STAY CONTENT JUST BEING A NORMAL ELEVEN-YEAR-OLD GIRL, TURN TO PAGE 109.**

➲ **TO FOLLOW IN YOUR MOTHER'S FOOTSTEPS AND GET REVENGE ON THE BRITISH FOR THROWING ETHAN IN PRISON, TURN TO PAGE 91.**

You don't know what went wrong. The information you sent to the Culper Ring should've forced them to find a way to save Ethan—saying he had secret intelligence that was vital to the war effort should've done the trick.

But as far as you can tell, no action has been taken.

You get the sense that Culper Ring knows you were trying to use them and you can't shake the feeling that your relationship with this elusive spy group is now over.

Future notes you send to them aren't responded to.

You never see Ethan again, either.

While loyal Patriots do their job and eventually help save America from British oppression, you don't play much of a part in it. Still, you survived the war and enjoyed an exciting but very brief career as a spy.

That's at least something.

THE END

The Continental Congress soon makes counterfeiting a capital crime. Anyone caught making it will be hanged. The Congress even offers a sizable reward for turning in counterfeiters.

You know this is in no small part due to what you uncovered and sent along to the Culper Ring. Huzzah, Agent 355! You're well on your way to helping America win this war with Great Britain.

➲ **TURN TO PAGE 42.**

CONTINENTAL CURRENCY
TWENTY DOLLARS
THIS BILL entitles the Bearer to
Twenty Dollars.
No.
4432
1775.

Aunt Myrtle knows plenty of officers, both Continental and British, and as a result, you've seen more than a few military documents of minor importance. Still, forging one isn't easy.

But what better way is there to suggest an attack is forthcoming than to have military orders saying it's so?

It takes many tries, but you finally create one that you think looks genuine. Anyone who sees it will believe General Washington is secretly staging a well-coordinated attack on New York City from the north and south.

Now you just need to let it "slip" into the hands of the British.

⮕ **TO LEAVE IT PARTIALLY HIDDEN IN THE NEARBY BURNED-OUT WAREHOUSE THE BRITISH ARE REPAIRING, TURN TO PAGE 82.**

⮕ **TO SLIP IT INTO THE CORRESPONDENCE OF A KNOWN LOYALIST SPY, TURN TO PAGE 88.**

America is well on its way to victory, freedom, and independence . . . thanks to George Washington, the Continental army, and brave patriots like those in the Culper Ring.

Only no one will ever know about the dangerous, daring work done by spies. Others might even take credit for what YOU risked your life to do.

That's okay.

Heroes aren't always recorded by history. But heroes are heroes, all the same.

Congratulations, Agent 355. Enjoy the quiet life of a young lady living in the country you helped free from British oppression.

You deserve it.

THE END

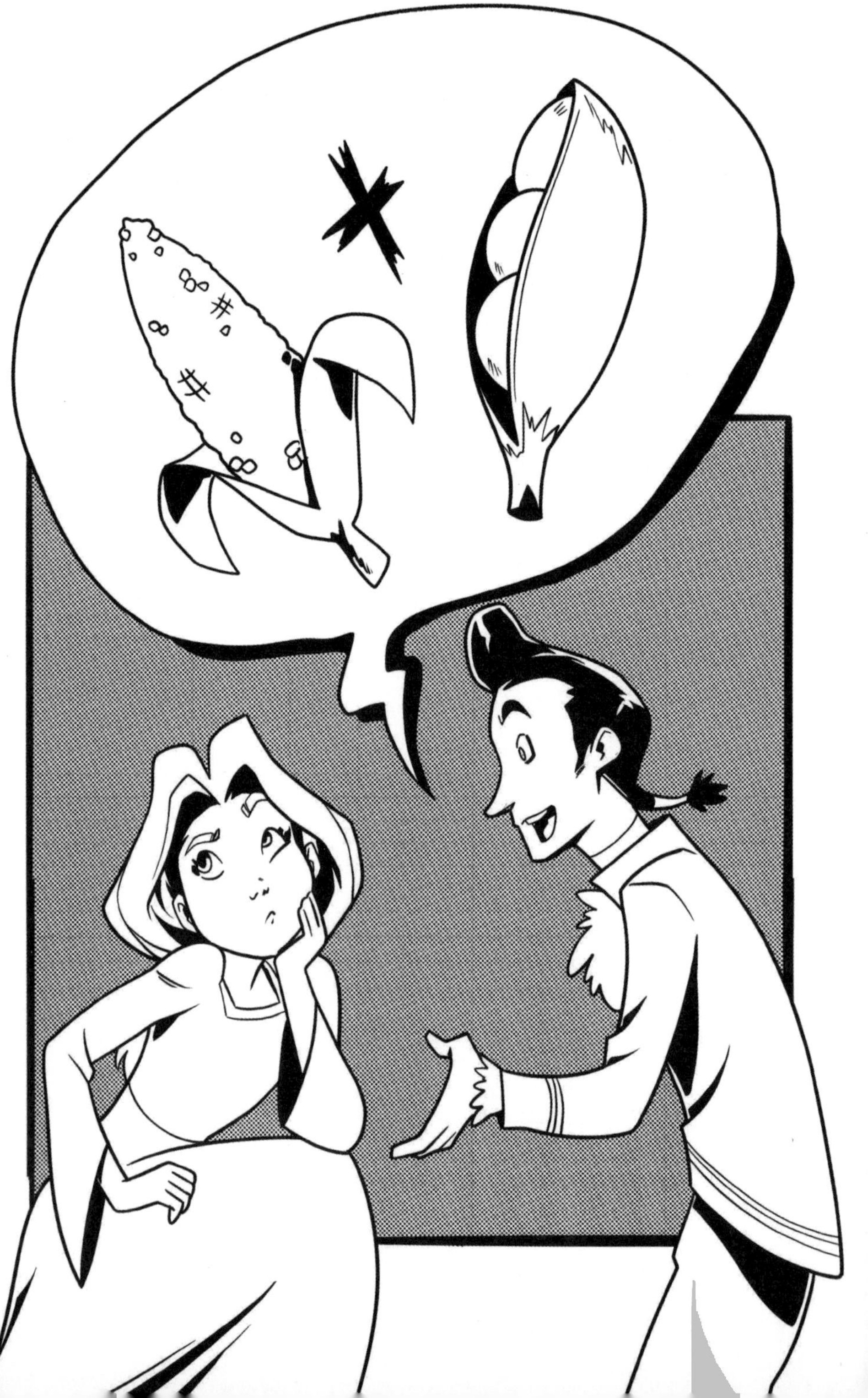

You try your best to befriend Michael, your second cousin who lives just a few blocks away, because his father's the type of man who knows all manner of important things about the British. Being near him might offer you all kinds of opportunities.

But Michael might be the most boring person you've ever met. All he wants to talk about is the role of religion in society. He's especially keen on discussing the influence of the Quakers on the Puritans far beyond the point where normal people are interested.

When you finally force him to change the topic, he drones on about intercropping, which is when someone plants two or more crops in the same field at the same time so one crop can support or provide shade for the other, such as growing corn and beans simultaneously.

Ugh.

There are limits to one's patience, Agent 355, and you've reached yours with Michael.

➲ **TO CREATE A PLAN TO RESCUE ETHAN FROM HIS PRISON SHIP, TURN TO PAGE 93.**

➲ **TO STAY PATIENT AND WAIT THE NEXT OPPORTUNITY FOR SPYING OR ACTION TO COME TO YOU, TURN TO PAGE 24.**

Decide & Survive: Agent 355

You listen at the door but because of a ruckus in the street, you can't hear if someone's inside the room or not.

You try the door. It's locked, but you easily work it open with a hairpin—you've been practicing.

"What's this?" hollers a voice. It's a man sitting at a desk stacked high with cash—more money than most see in a lifetime. Enough to fill a wheelbarrow.

When the man realizes you're just a girl and not the constable or a troop of soldiers, he growls and charges. He's as big as a bear and he's roaring toward you.

This isn't turning out the way you hoped. Spies are better at sneaking, not fighting.

You leap aside just in time. The bristle-chinned man crashes into an end table, which bursts into splinters. You grab a broken table leg and slam it against his back. Once, twice, three times.

He doesn't get up.

Was your fight too loud? Is Mr. Muller or another lodger coming to check?

⊃ **TO QUICKLY GRAB WHAT YOU CAN AND FLEE, TURN TO PAGE 80.**

⊃ **TO CAREFULLY SCOUR THE ROOM TO GET TO THE BOTTOM OF THIS COUNTERFEIT MONEY THREAT, TURN TO PAGE 40.**

Months later, the war remains a stalemate. Sometimes the newspapers suggest that the British are winning. Sometimes they report that the Colonials have the upper hand. It's a tense time. No one's quite sure what to believe, though New York remains firmly in the tight grasp of the British.

During this period, the new governess Aunt Myrtle insisted on getting is teaching you etiquette, dance, and French. The first two lessons don't interest you much, but knowing another language seems quite useful for spy work.

You soon become *très* good at French!

When you're not hard at work with your lessons, you continue to attend parties, stop by eating houses, and browse the open-air markets, listening and learning all you can. A spy needs to be out in the world, paying attention. You never know when something useful might happen right in front of you.

➲ **TURN TO PAGE 97.**

You engage in small talk with the other guests while waiting for your chance. When Benedict Arnold accepts a snifter of brandy from a serving boy and heads onto the porch to enjoy it beneath the stars, you follow.

"I know about West Point," you say.

He's startled, but he regains his composure so quickly that you're not sure you saw him falter. His blue coat has gold trim that catches the starlight, as do the silver buckles on his shoes. He's such a stylish dresser that it's almost hard to believe he's a general.

"And just what do you think you know?"

"Enough to ruin you."

He sips his brandy. "Don't you ever wonder what it'd be like to be on the winning side? For once in your life?"

"The British don't have a chance because—"

"The British ALWAYS win," he says. Then he leans close. "And you can be part of it, little spy."

You thought you were so clever with all your spying, but as Benedict Arnold talks to you in the hush of night on the porch, it's clear both he and Major André know all about the Culper Ring. And you, too. You figure the next thing he'll do is holler for the guards and have you thrown in prison.

But he doesn't. Instead, he makes you the offer of a lifetime.

➲ **TO HAND OVER YOUR MOM'S CODEBOOK AND STAY SILENT ABOUT THE WEST POINT PLANS IN RETURN FOR £10,000, TURN TO PAGE 71.**

➲ **TO REFUSE TO BETRAY AMERICA AND THE CULPER RING, TURN TO PAGE 46.**

The door isn't locked, so your kick smashes it open.

"Aha!" you cry, pointing at the man sitting at a desk stacked high with cash—more money than most see in a lifetime. Enough to fill a wheelbarrow.

When the man realizes you're just a girl and not the constable or a troop of soldiers, he growls and charges. He's as big as a bear and he's roaring toward you.

This isn't turning out the way you'd hoped. Spies are better at sneaking, not fighting.

You leap aside just in time. The bristle-chinned man crashes into an end table, which bursts into splinters. You grab a broken table leg and slam it against his back. Once, twice, three times.

He doesn't get up.

Was your fight too loud? Is Mr. Muller or another lodger coming to check?

➲ **TO QUICKLY GRAB WHAT YOU CAN AND FLEE, TURN TO PAGE 80.**

➲ **TO CAREFULLY SCOUR THE ROOM TO GET TO THE BOTTOM OF THIS COUNTERFEIT MONEY THREAT, TURN TO PAGE 40.**

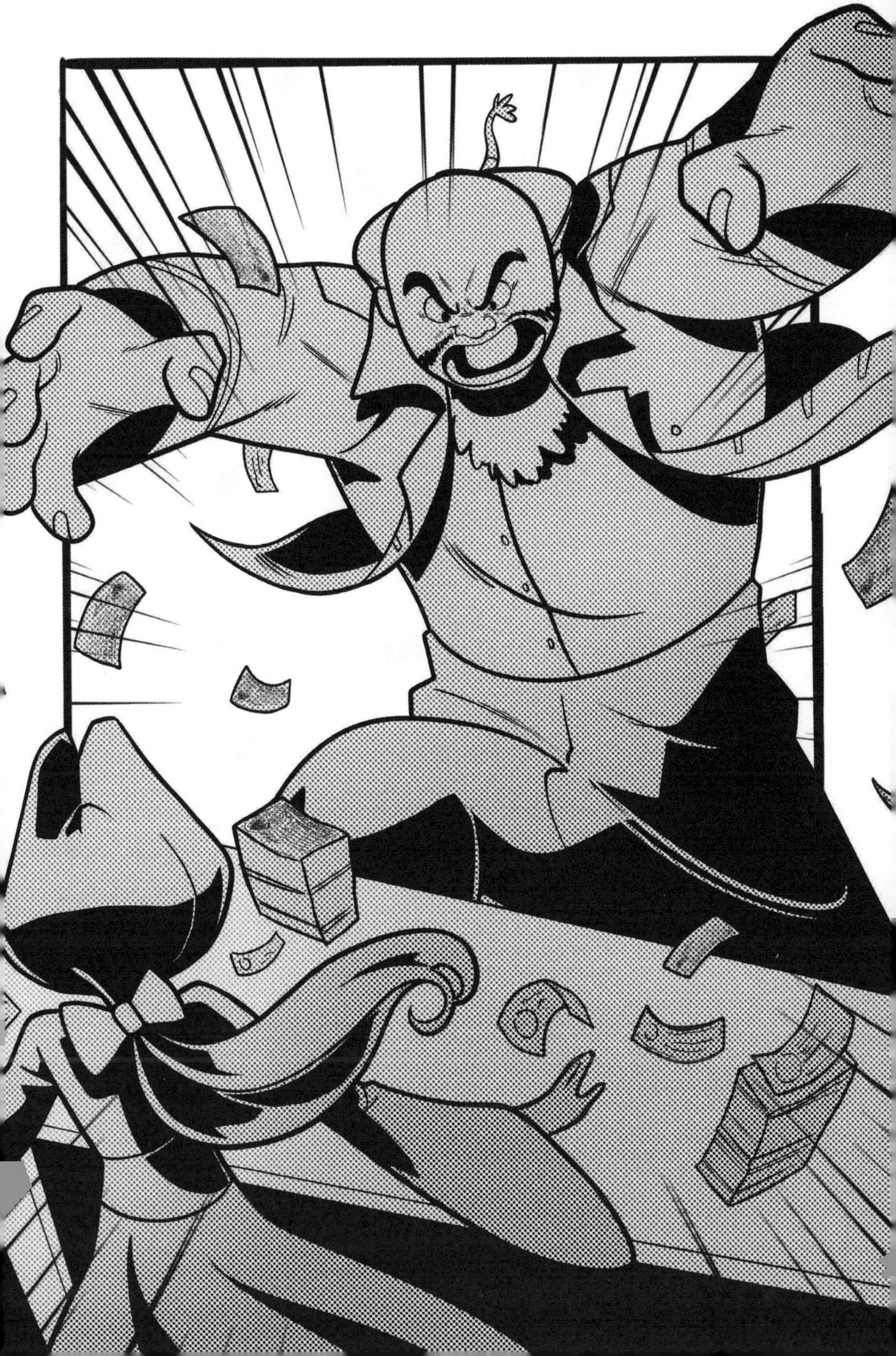

You scramble into the underbrush to hide.

Did they see you?

Do they hear your heartbeat hammering away?

Can they smell the sweat dampening your bonnet?

Gloved hands reach through the thick green of boxwood bushes. You try to run, but it's too late.

"Another rebel spying on troop movements?" bellows an officer. It's one of the men from the party who boasted about George Washington's impending death. He doesn't recognize you in the shabby maid's outfit.

"No, sir," you say. "I was just . . ."

He laughs. "Take her to the prison ship with the rest. The gents on the HMS *Strombolo* will ferret the truth out of this little bird."

You don't like the sound of that, but what can you do? There's no point fighting—a dozen muskets could fire within moments.

Spies have patience. Wait for your time to act.

⮕ **TURN TO PAGE 13.**

Sometimes a spy must get extremely creative to get the job done, and by finding this hidden page, you've done exactly that!

You don't know how this happens, but you look down and find Harry Potter's 11" holly wand in your hand. Don't ask how or why. Just put it to good use!

With a flick of your wrist, BOOM, the walls of the prison ship holding Ethan crumble to dust. A few more flicks of the powerful wand remove the prisoners' chains, create inflatable unicorn boats for each of them, and send the stunned British guards flipping head over feet into the far side of the bay.

You and Ethan embrace. He's as skinny as a willow branch and he positively reeks. "Zippity dippity do!" you whisper as you wiggle the wand, and WHAM, he's clean and healthy as he used to be. He whoops with joy.

"Hey," Ethan says after a moment. He points. "What's that?"

You look at the huge crate behind you. There's no way to know without opening it, so you pry off the lid. Inside are fifty *Star Trek* phasers that fire nadion particle beams that can disrupt or destroy targets.

You pass them out to the escaped prisoners and tell them each to "Set phasers to stun!" Afterward, with your superior firepower and the incredible story-altering magic of your wand, you drive every one of those British intruders straight out of the colonies for good.

You've saved the day, Agent 355. America owes you a huge debt of gratitude.

Not bad for taking a little chance, right?

THE END

You did it! Because of the fake information you spread, General Clinton keeps the British army back at New York City . . . for an attack that never comes.

Admiral Chevalier de Ternay and his 6,000 French soldiers arrive safely in America, which gives the British a second army to worry about.

Another success, Agent 355. Of course, no one knows to thank you, but that's just the life of a spy.

➲ **TURN TO PAGE 61.**

Some of the other prisoners hunker behind a wagon, too scared to run.

Not you.

A spy knows when to wait and when to take action. And the time to do the latter is now. RUN!

You yank up your woolen skirt and charge into the woods, away from the battle. A branch smacks you in the face and you trip twice, but you get up and keep going because your life—quite literally—depends on it.

The thundering cracks of musket fire eventually dwindle to nothing. It's just you and the quiet hush of the forest.

You still need to deliver your message and you're pretty sure you've got quite a few miles to go. Your stomach growls as you hurry down an old hunting trail, which allows you to pick up a bit of speed. The turnips you brought for a snack fell out during your escape, and the wild blueberry bushes have been nibbled clean by deer, squirrels, and bears, if the tracks are any indication.

With luck, you won't run into another British patrol.

You grit your teeth and continue toward the secret place where your mother's codebook said you could leave a message for a Culper courier.

⮕ **TURN TO PAGE 102.**

"Thank you, thank you," you find yourself saying over and over to the lords and ladies of London, which is your new home. Everyone wants to meet the Lady Who Defeated America. Even King George III met with you personally to bestow riches upon you by way of thanks for helping defeat the upstart Patriots.

As nice as it is to live in a huge British mansion and have endless closets full of clothes, more servants than you know what to do with, and the fawning attention of everyone you meet, you can't help but wonder: What would've happened had you stayed true to the Culper Ring and fought to the very end for the American cause? Was all of this worth having your name recorded in the history books as one of the biggest traitors of all time, right alongside Brutus, Judas Iscariot, and Guy Fawkes?

THE END

Aunt Myrtle might've threatened to keep you on a short leash in the city, but as the days go by, she gets busier and busier with friends, parties, and shopping. Even with your own duties helping to manage the household in the two-story wooden building in Manhattan, you have ample time to roam about.

Even when there's nothing to report, being a spy is dangerous. British soldiers are quartered in nearly every inn, boarding house, and home in the city. You spend many evenings at The Brown Horse Inn down by the waterfront, where you sip cranberry juice and occasionally play parlor games with one of the baker's sons as you scan the crowd and listen.

No one warned you that being a spy could be so boring!

After three weeks of nothing happening, you wonder if you should take action. Any action!

⇨ **TO CREATE A PLAN TO RESCUE ETHAN FROM HIS PRISON SHIP, TURN TO PAGE 93.**

⇨ **TO STAY PATIENT, TURN TO PAGE 24.**

⇨ **TO BEFRIEND MICHAEL, WHOSE FATHER IS A HIGH-RANKING GOVERNMENT LOYALIST, TURN TO PAGE 59.**

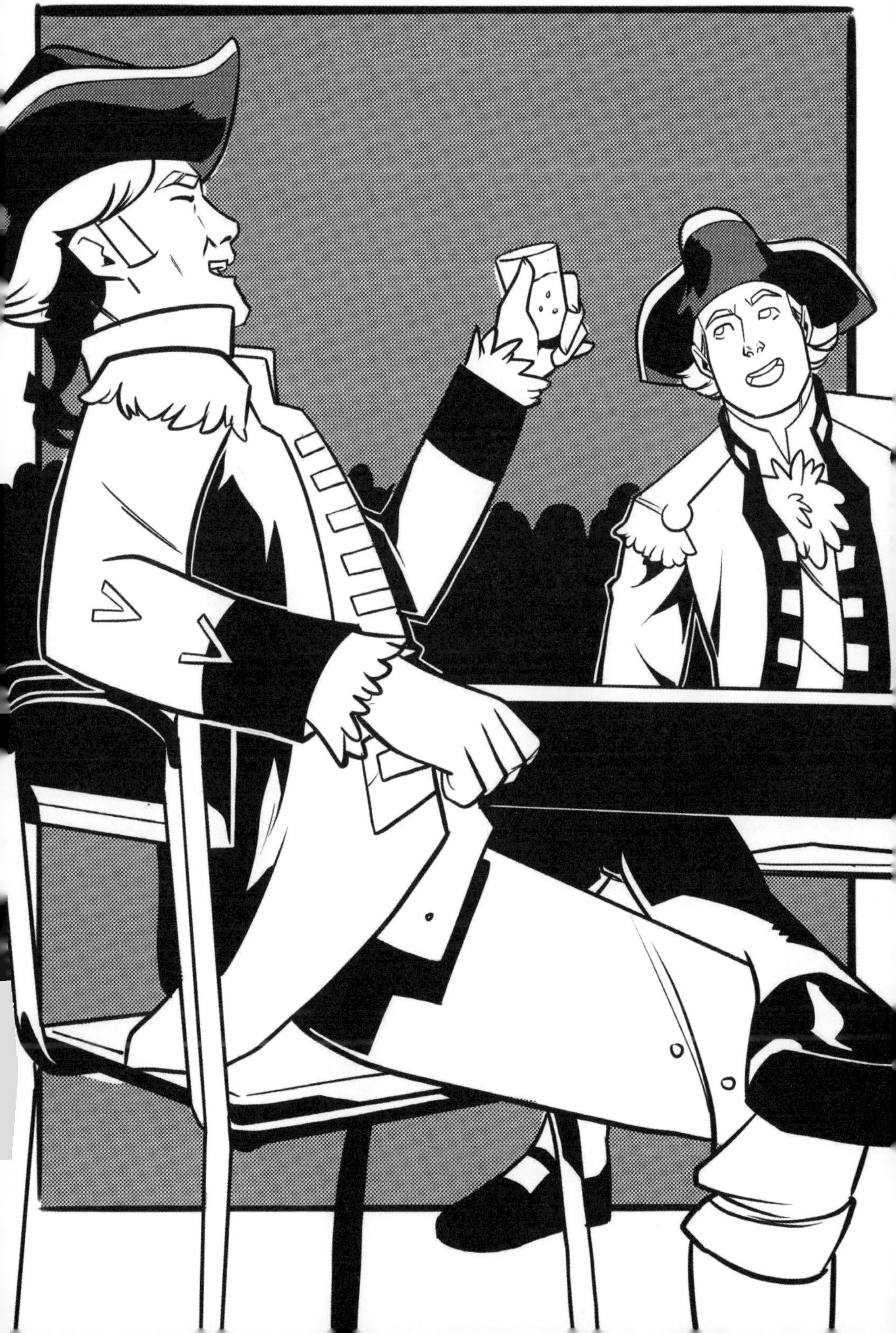

Thanks to the heads-up you passed along, General Washington must've uncovered the traitor in his camp because he's still alive. Without your help, the Continental army would've lost its leader.

Go home and rest up, Agent 355. You have more work to do. You didn't think it'd be this easy to save an entire nation, did you?

General Washington's army is still outnumbered and outsupplied. Keeping him informed of British plans and troop movements is vital to the Patriot cause.

Above all, don't get caught. The punishment for spying is death by hanging—just like what happened to Nathan Hale, one of Washington's spies before the Culper Ring existed.

➲ **TURN TO PAGE 15.**

These robbers are soldiers. Their hair is matted and tangled, and their deep-set eyes and sunken cheeks speak of long, hard days on the road.

They're no match for a Culper Ring spy!

With a whoop, you leap atop the seat of the nearest wagon and kick the horse into action. Like a cannonball fired from a British frigate, you zoom toward the robbers. This is the type of heroic story you'll tell your grandkids in front of a roaring fire someday!

Only the robbers are following the plotline of a different story, and it's one where they don't scatter and flee like a bunch of cowards but instead stand their ground and open fire.

Your last thought is that it's more than a little ironic that you gave your life not to save America but to protect a Loyalist and a handful of servants. Not the worst reason to die, sure, but this wasn't the outcome you'd imagined.

THE END

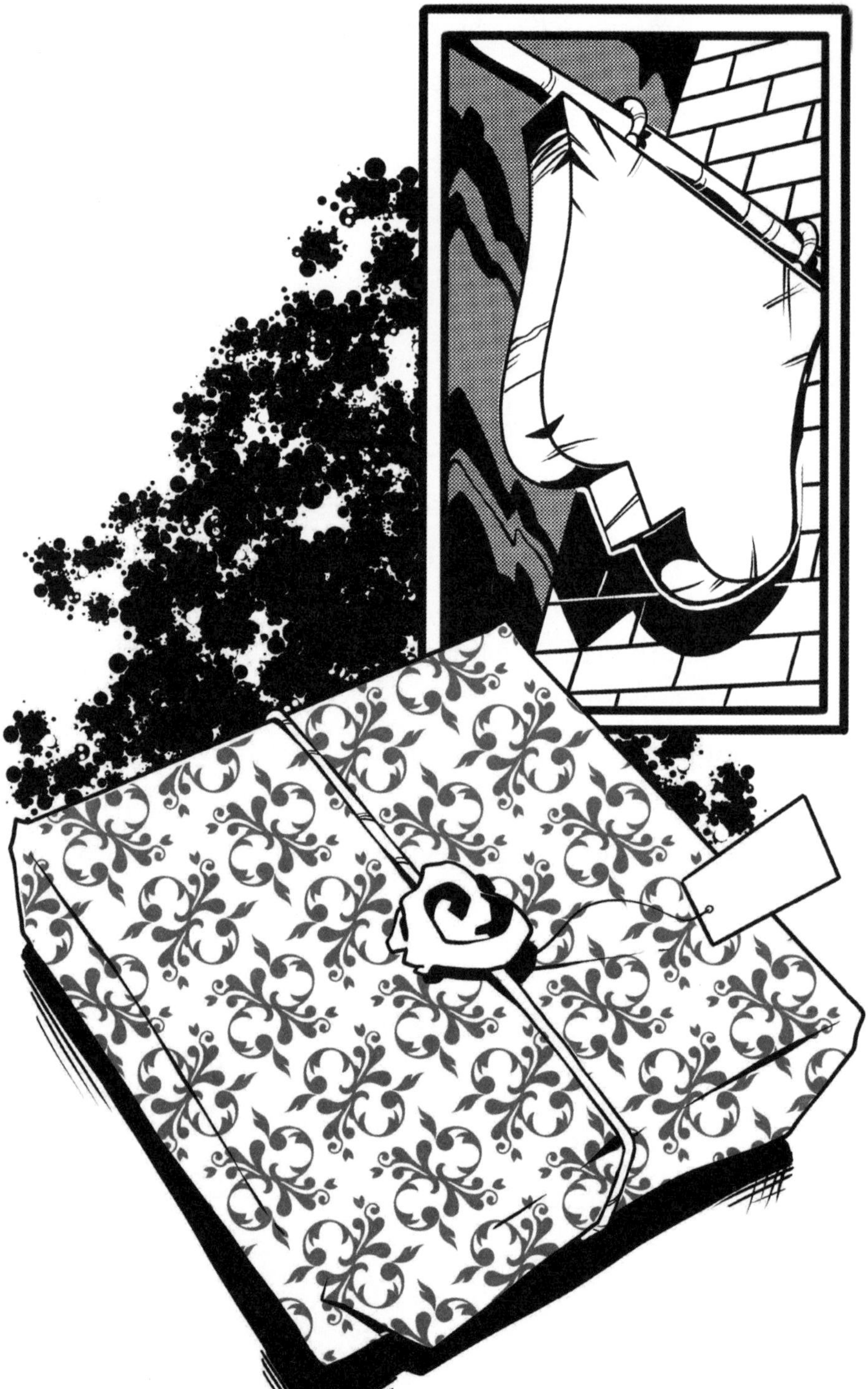

After dinner a few nights later, Aunt Myrtle tells you to deliver a birthday present to a dear friend of hers who's staying at The Plough and Harrow. You like that inn—they have the best fish chowder around—so you happily agree.

You smell fresh-cut onions and salt pork even before you enter the busy main room. Your mouth waters.

"This is for Penelope Wood!" you shout to the innkeeper, a lean-faced man with a dirty apron. "It's a present from my aunt."

You think his name is Elijah, but he doesn't even look up from his plate-washing. Instead, he just nods to the stairs. "Third door to the left."

Up you go, moving to the side on the stairs to let a gray-bearded British officer past without so much as a "Thank you!"

Penelope doesn't answer even when you pound. But across the hall, you see that rude officer's door is slightly ajar. No one's around, so you nudge it open with your foot.

Is that a half-written letter there on the desk? You leave Penelope's gift outside her door while you ponder your options.

➲ **TO SNEAK INSIDE THE OFFICER'S ROOM AND CHECK OUT THAT LETTER, TURN TO PAGE 49.**

➲ **TO QUIT TEMPTING FORTUNE AND HEAD HOME WITHOUT INVESTIGATING FURTHER, TURN TO PAGE 87.**

You wait until the following evening so you have time to properly plan for your raid on the prison ship. No one warned you what it'd actually be like once you slipped into the dark waters of Wallabout Bay, though. The current yanks you in every direction at once. Waves crash over you, making it hard to say afloat.

Keeping hold of your waxed canvas bag full of tools is nearly impossible. It takes all your strength to keep from being swept away.

You head back to shore and reconsider the wisdom of this plan. There on the shore, you shiver in the night air, your waterlogged cotton dress clinging to you like a glove.

➲ **TO GIVE UP RESCUING ETHAN ON YOUR OWN, TURN TO PAGE 24.**

➲ **TO STEAL A BOAT AND ROW OUT TO SAVE ETHAN, TURN TO PAGE 44.**

As you suspected, the paper money is fake. That's interesting.

You turn your efforts to the note and ledger. Both are in code, but a few hours later, you solve that puzzle. The British are behind the counterfeit money! They're flooding the colonies with fake money to destroy the American economy.

If Continental money is worthless, Continental soldiers can't be paid. If they can't be paid, they surely won't fight no matter how much they believe in the Patriot cause.

This is a disaster!

You leave samples of the fake currency along with a coded message to your contact at a drop-off point beneath a bridge outside the city. You alert the Culper Ring by marking a small X on a specific brick in the rear of a Quaker meeting house.

➲ **TURN TO PAGE 54.**

Decide & Survive: Agent 355

A spy knows when to stay and when to flee. Your brain is screaming RUN!

Yet you need information, too. So, you grab a stack of cash along with a ledger you notice on the desk. You pause to check the downed man. In a jacket pocket, he has a note written in code.

Heavy footsteps on the stairs confirm your fear—trouble is on the way!

You slide open the second-story window and wiggle out onto the flagstone chimney. You barely get the window shut before someone enters the room. Golden lantern light touches your face through the smoked glass. You duck away.

Did they see you?

Stay calm, Agent 355. Take a slow, deep breath. Thankfully, there are few streetlamps in this part of the city, so passersby don't notice you hanging against the chimney.

The room lights eventually go off.

You climb down and hurry home. Soon, you'll be able to check through what you found in the safety of your own bedroom.

⮕ **TURN TO PAGE 79.**

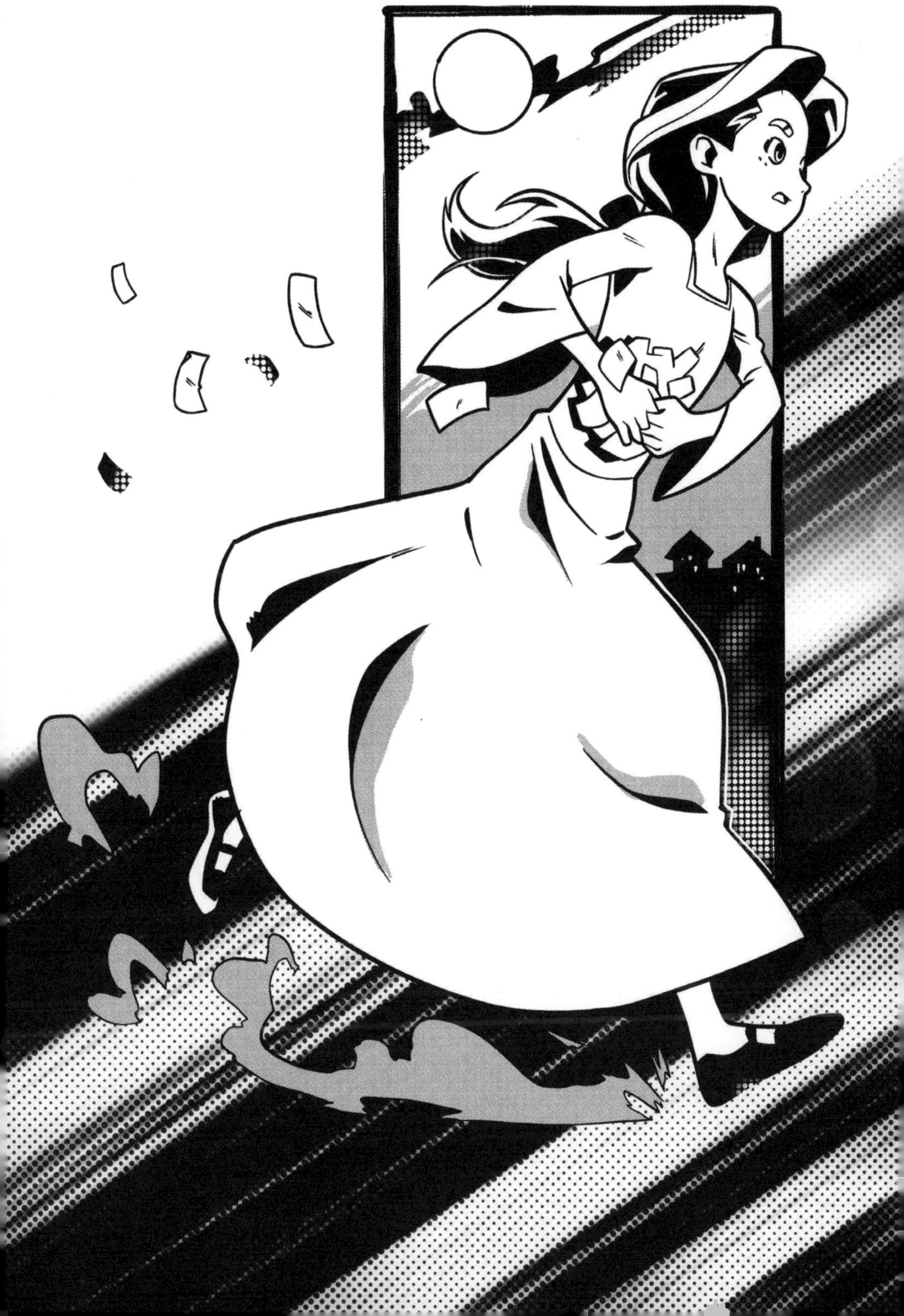

During a storm two weeks back, a lightning strike set the Wilson's inn and barn aflame. Just a few days ago, British soldiers and Loyalists began rebuilding it since its proximity to the harbor made it an ideal site for a supply depot. Mr. Wilson, a vocal critic of the crown, complained about the soldiers confiscating his property, damaged or not.

He hasn't been seen since.

With so many British soldiers and Loyalists around that construction site, you suspect it's a perfect place to "hide" your forged document in a way that it could be discovered. People might easily believe that poor Mr. Wilson was involved in the rebellion and that the document was his.

As you've learned to do anytime you're on Culper Ring business, you take a roundabout path. It takes twice as long, but you can never be too safe.

Since you're disguised as a commoner, the woman cooking lamb stew for the workers doesn't mind speaking with you. Without your silks and lace, no one would guess that your guardian is the wealthy Loyalist Myrtle Walker. The secondhand shoes you borrowed from a servant and your third-oldest bonnet help sell the disguise.

One of the British soldiers lingers near the stewpot,

asking the cook about the weather and the recent cabbage shortage.

Is he suspicious? Bored? Avoiding work?

You have a job to do, though. You must save the French navy!

➲ **TO TUCK THE FAKE MILITARY DOCUMENT BY THE LUMBER PILE, TURN TO PAGE 34.**

➲ **TO DELIVER IT TO THE SOLDIER WITH A FAKE STORY ABOUT HOW YOU DISCOVERED IT, TURN TO PAGE 106.**

With the highwaymen in chains at the hands of Captain Wilford and his men, you're safe. Aunt Myrtle thanks the handsome captain profusely. You swallow your disgust and do the same.

"This rabble isn't the only trouble we've found on the roads today," he says. He adjusts his sheathed sword as he glares at the robbers, who no longer seem all that ferocious. In fact, they seem like desperate people who are a few days from starvation.

"Oh dear," says one of Aunt Myrtle's maids.

Captain Wilford holds up his hand. "I insist we ride with you, ladies. At least as far as Jamaica."

And so, for the remainder of your journey westward, you have a British guard. Unfortunately, nothing they say or do is of interest to you as a spy.

There's a moment of excitement when General Charles Grey arrives with a contingent of more than a thousand people heading to Fort St. George. Your group moves off the dirt road to allow them to pass. You watch in awe at all the soldiers and the dozens of civilians who support this small army. Laundresses, musicians, sutlers, nurses, cooks, blacksmiths, and others you aren't quite sure what they do. Wow.

When the last of them finally goes past, your group resumes its own journey.

When you reach a British encampment outside Jamaica a few hours later, the small group of British soldiers that saved you finally take their leave.

"You'll have an easy route ahead," says the captain. "The roads from here on are well patrolled, as you'll no doubt see for yourself."

"Thank you for all of your help," Aunt Myrtle says. "And god save the king."

"God save the king!" shout the soldiers.

➲ **TURN TO PAGE 48.**

You're furious over Ethan rotting away in a prison ship and equally angry about so many things you've witnessed the British do back on Long Island and here in the city. Enough is enough.

You grab an empty wine bottle and face off against the British soldiers along with dozens of other grim-faced Patriots armed with makeshift weapons and fueled by their passion for independence. You outnumber the soldiers three to one.

Those are good odds, right?

But wine bottles, chairs, and rocks are no match for pistols, muskets, and bayonets.

As you bleed out on the cobblestones, you wonder if the French are truly coming and if it'll be the tipping point of the war. You sure hope so.

THE END

Further down the hall, another guest's door creaks open. You don't want to be caught standing right outside the half-open door of a British officer's room, so you do the first thing that comes to mind. You duck inside and close the door behind you.

You hear someone walk down the hall and go down the stairs. After twenty heartbeats, you decide it's probably safe to leave.

Yet you're already in the room, so you might as well read the letter.

➲ **TURN TO PAGE 49.**

Hudson Valley Butchers is where Cook buys fatback for frying pork chops and all the ingredients for Aunt Myrtle's favorite—veal potpie. Eight people wait in line to make their purchases. The clink of metal and the smell of fresh meat and sawdust fill your senses.

You linger in the back, waiting for your chance.

There on the counter is a stack of fresh mail waiting for the postman. The Culper Ring knows that this butcher, a Loyalist spy, regularly sends correspondence to Major André and other members of the British Army's Secret Service. Anything that leaves in the mail will be seen by British spies. What better way to get the word out about Washington's fake assault?

When the butcher hollers at a mother for allowing her child to poke at a slab of fresh bacon, you act. The exact moment you slide your false document into the mail, a man beside you says, "Excuse me."

You freeze. Were you just caught?

The man's dressed in a plain linen shirt with a high collar and cuffs, and his well-worn leather boots have clearly seen many miles of serious use. He's no soldier, but behind the thin spectacles on his nose, his eyes are disturbingly sharp and observant.

"Yes?" you say. It's hard to keep your voice from breaking.

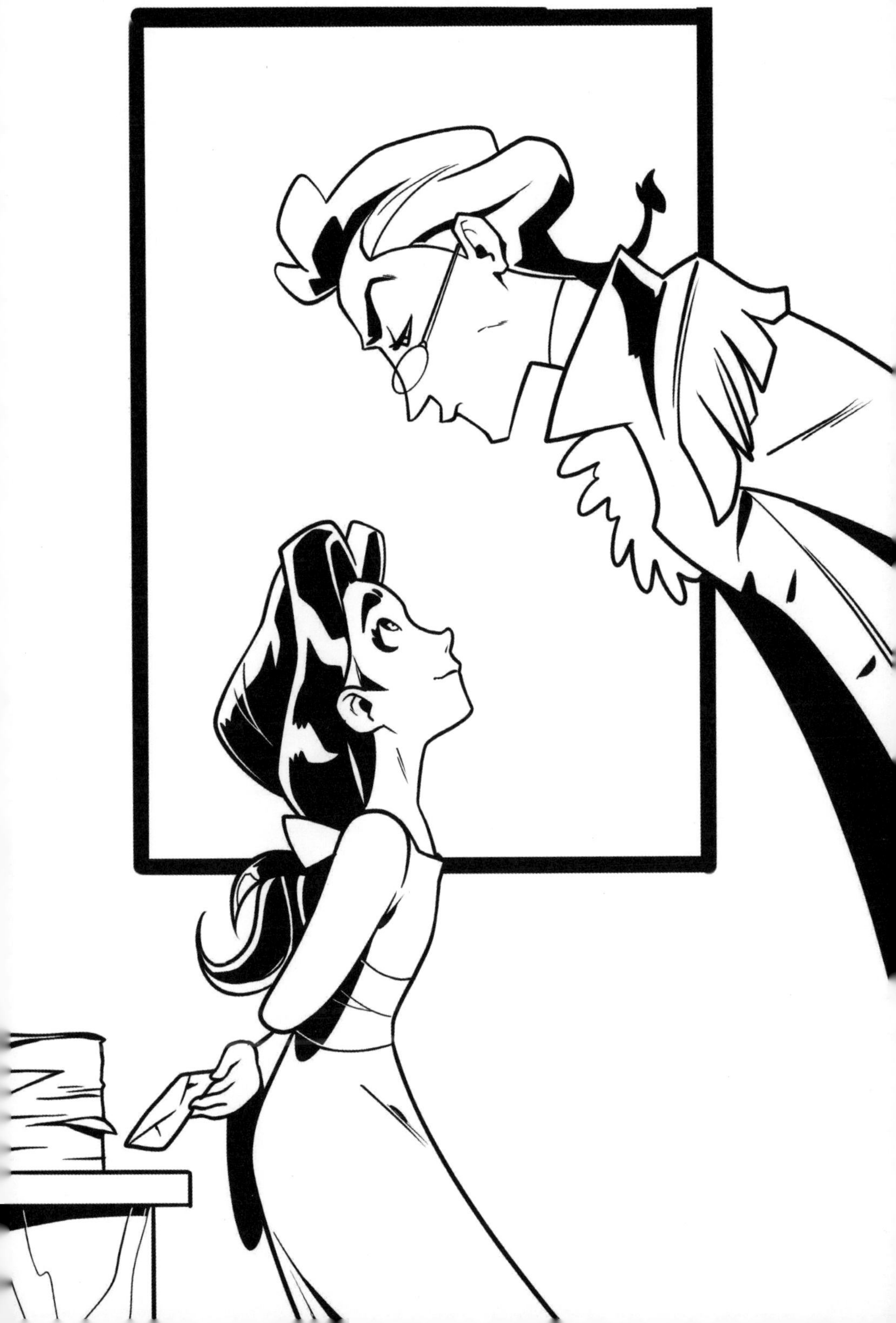

He frowns. "Have you ever had the peppered ham? Is it better than the smoked ham here? I haven't been to this shop before."

You feel the tension release from you body. "The peppered ham is absolutely delightful," you assure him.

➲ **TURN TO PAGE 69.**

Aunt Myrtle's house is alive with conversation and laughter. The British soldiers are in fancy red uniforms, and the British sympathizers are decked out in the finest Colonial-style clothing, with powdered wigs and flowing dresses for the ladies and embroidered waistcoats and tri-cornered hats for the men. The food is extravagant—roasted quail, buttered walnut biscuits, and turtledove pie. The drinks are just as plentiful, with a variety of imported wines and ales from the British Isles.

In one corner of the room, a group of musicians plays traditional melodies on the fiddle, mandolin, and guitar. Guests clap and sing along to the music, enjoying the festive atmosphere.

You move from room to room, helping the servants collect empty plates and mugs. No one pays that much attention to them or you. Not even when you walk into a study and two British officers laugh about how General Washington will soon be dead at the hands of his own special guard.

You must warn him!

The two soldiers barely look at you as you curtsy and exit the room, leaving them to their drinking, merriment, and scheming.

⮕ **TO HANG LAUNDRY ON THE LINE IN A CODED MANNER TO SUMMON A CULPER COURIER, TURN TO PAGE 95.**

⮕ **TO DELIVER THIS IMPORTANT INFORMATION YOURSELF, TURN TO PAGE 26.**

"Take a shawl with you," Aunt Myrtle says as you head out. "It's cold!"

You do, though you're so excited by the prospect of rescuing Ethan that the night air wouldn't have bothered you in the least, with or without a shawl.

It took you six days to learn the identity of the former British soldier who sometimes sold military information to Patriots for the right price. It took another week to set up a meeting—which is tonight at The Rooster, a lousy eating house on the south side of the city.

A rat skitters past as you step into the shadowy main room.

There in the corner sits the scar-chinned man you're looking for. You settle into the chair across from him. He spoons boiled turnips into his mouth while he nods as you.

"Whaddya want?"

You check. No one is paying attention. Still, there's no need to be careless, so you lean close.

"The name of the prison ship holding Ethan Miller," you whisper as you slide across your mother's favorite broach, a pretty gold and ivory item that's the most valuable thing you have. You hate giving it up, but while Aunt Myrtle buys you what you need, she doesn't give you money. This is the only way to bribe a man like this into helping you.

The man makes the broach disappear into his pocket.

"The HMS *Scorpion*. In Wallabout Bay."

"Thank you," you say.

The man grunts and chews his turnips.

➲ **TO SWIM OUT TO THE PRISON SHIP UNDER THE COVER OF DARK, TURN TO PAGE 78.**

➲ **TO SEND FAKE INFORMATION TO THE CULPER RING THAT'LL MAKE THEM WANT TO RESCUE ETHAN THEMSELVES, TURN TO PAGE 53.**

It's hard to imagine how hanging laundry on the outside line of your old house in a specific way—colors, patterns, etc.—is a way to communicate with the Culper Ring, but that's what your codebook says.

The next morning, the winds of Long Island are too blustery for hanging laundry. Plus, your old house has new Loyalist occupants who wouldn't understand you putting up laundry in their backyard anyway. Even if you somehow convinced them to let you hang laundry, you can't wait for good weather with General Washington's life in peril. He's the key to the entire American Revolution!

There's only one choice—pass on the information about the assassination attempt yourself in one of the other ways outlined in your codebook.

➲ **TURN TO PAGE 26.**

There's not much room to write a coded note that fits inside a hollowed-out button of a dress, but you manage. You drag the dress through the dirt outside, and then drop it off at the home of a Patriot washerwoman. You know she'll pass the note along the Culper network.

Word comes back down through the Culper Ring—Benedict Arnold IS a traitor. He was willing to surrender West Point for a position in the British army and a small fortune.

General Washington now has him on the run. The entire Revolutionary War is now turning in favor of America. It's only a matter of time before the British lose their grip on the colonies.

Way to act at the right time, Agent 355.

➔ **TURN TO PAGE 57.**

A week after your twelfth birthday, you enter your favorite clothing store to buy yourself a treat with some of the birthday money given to you by Aunt Myrtle. When the milliner gives your change, you realize the money's . . . wrong.

The ink is off. The paper, too.

"Where did you get this?" you ask.

"A fisherman came through yesterday," the saleswoman says. "He spent a month's salary without a care in the world."

You recall hearing about a wild-spending man from the docks before but never thought much about it. Until now. Is someone distributing fake money?

This could be something important, Agent 355. Maybe other store owners have more information.

⇨ **TURN TO PAGE 18.**

It takes you a few weeks before you get the chance to get near Major André or Benedict Arnold, and by then, it's too late. West Point has fallen, and the Continental forces are in trouble. Day after day, General Washington loses more troops.

Eventually, General Cornwallis accepts the American surrender in Philadelphia. General Washington is imprisoned. The Culper Ring vanishes. The rebellion is over.

It's not easy for Patriots like you to be subjects of King George III, who doesn't mind taxing America increasingly more as punishment for the costly war. One by one, new laws restrict your freedom more and more.

Maybe things might've been different if you'd chosen a different path. Maybe not.

THE END

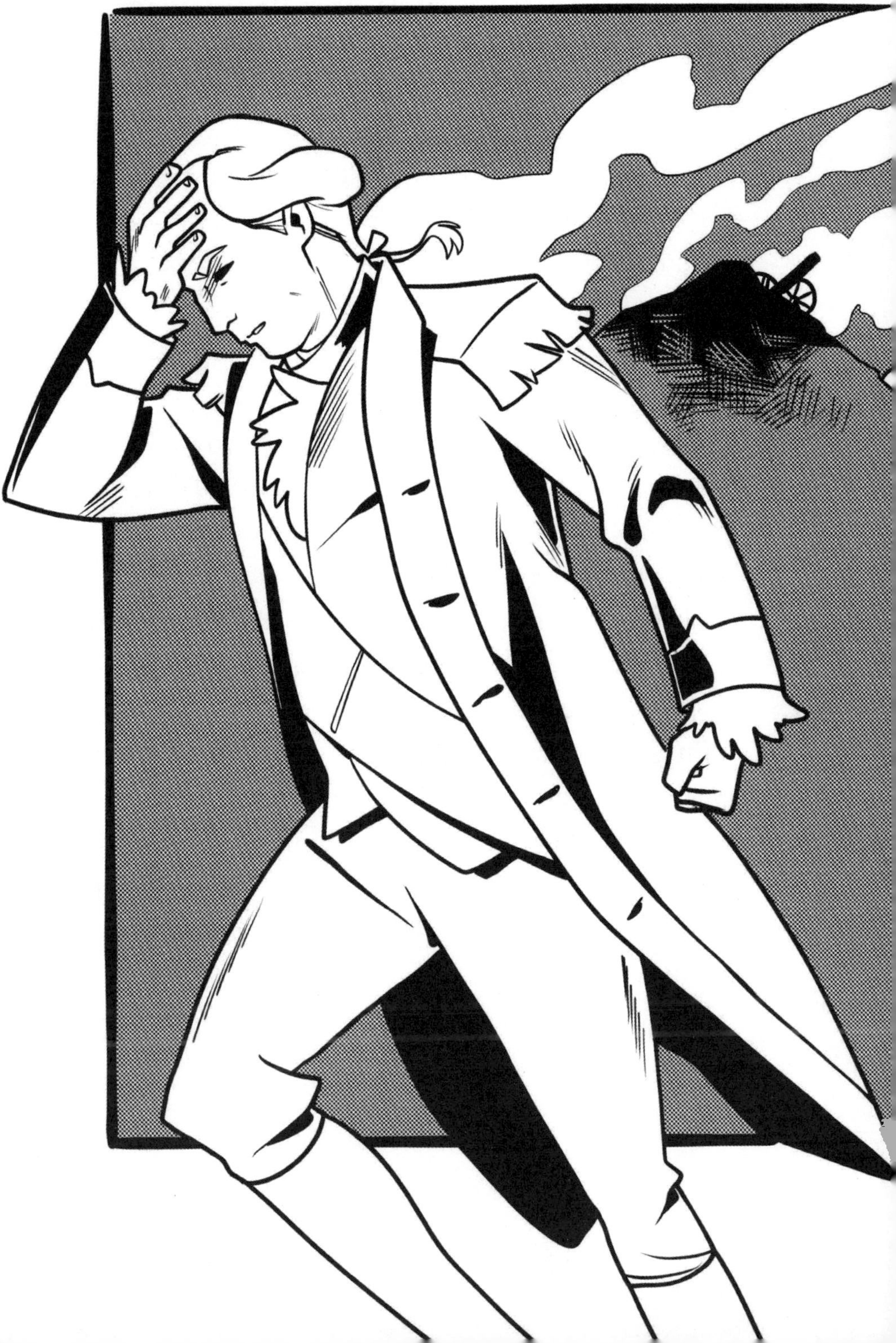

"Isn't General Washington's army in a stalemate with General Cornwallis?" Benjamin wonders when you ask for his help. "How could he get his army free of that and come to New York in time?"

You almost tell him a lie, but Benjamin's smile wins you over. You let him know that it's a ruse.

"A ruse? How would you know about a ruse? What are you, a spy or something?"

You realize you've said too much, so you tell him to forget the whole thing. "Sometimes you're really quite odd," he says, then he laughs and heads off to help Cook dice potatoes for dinner.

"That was a close one," you say, and you take it upon yourself to spread gossip about the fake attack. People seem to believe it.

But when General Cornwallis's troops miraculously appear at the French navy's landing site and rout the incoming troops, you realize something has gone terribly wrong. Exactly what happened becomes even more clear when troops arrive to arrest you for being involved in a rebellion.

Who'd have thought that kind-hearted, sweet Benjamin was a Loyalist spy?

THE END

You know better than to go head-to-head with British soldiers. People might be excited by the idea of the French joining the fight, but this isn't the time to become a martyr.

You hurry home and lock the door behind you.

Maybe the war is close to being over. Maybe not.

All you can do is wait and see if there's an opportunity for you to do your part to make the British pay for all they've done.

➲ **TURN TO PAGE 77.**

Decide & Survive: Agent 355

Your forehead is damp with sweat by the time you finally arrive at the destination you learned about from the codebook—a deep, dark cave near Stony Brook Harbor.

A high-pitched whistle sets your nerves on edge, but you know it's just one of the many ospreys you've seen in the woods throughout Long Island. When they feed, they warn off other animals by using a harsh, cracking call. Other times, they let out this noise, which sounded a bit too much like a person's shriek or scream.

You force yourself to be calm as you enter the cave.

The limestone cave is so cold that its walls are iced over even though it's summer. You puff into your hands for warmth and keep going deeper. In the very rear of the cave, you write a coded warning on the wall with chalk, just as the codebook explained.

A red handkerchief tied high in a poplar tree outside will alert your contact. A Culper spy courier will be along soon.

MISSION ACCOMPLISHED! Well done, Agent 355.

➲ **TURN TO PAGE 74.**

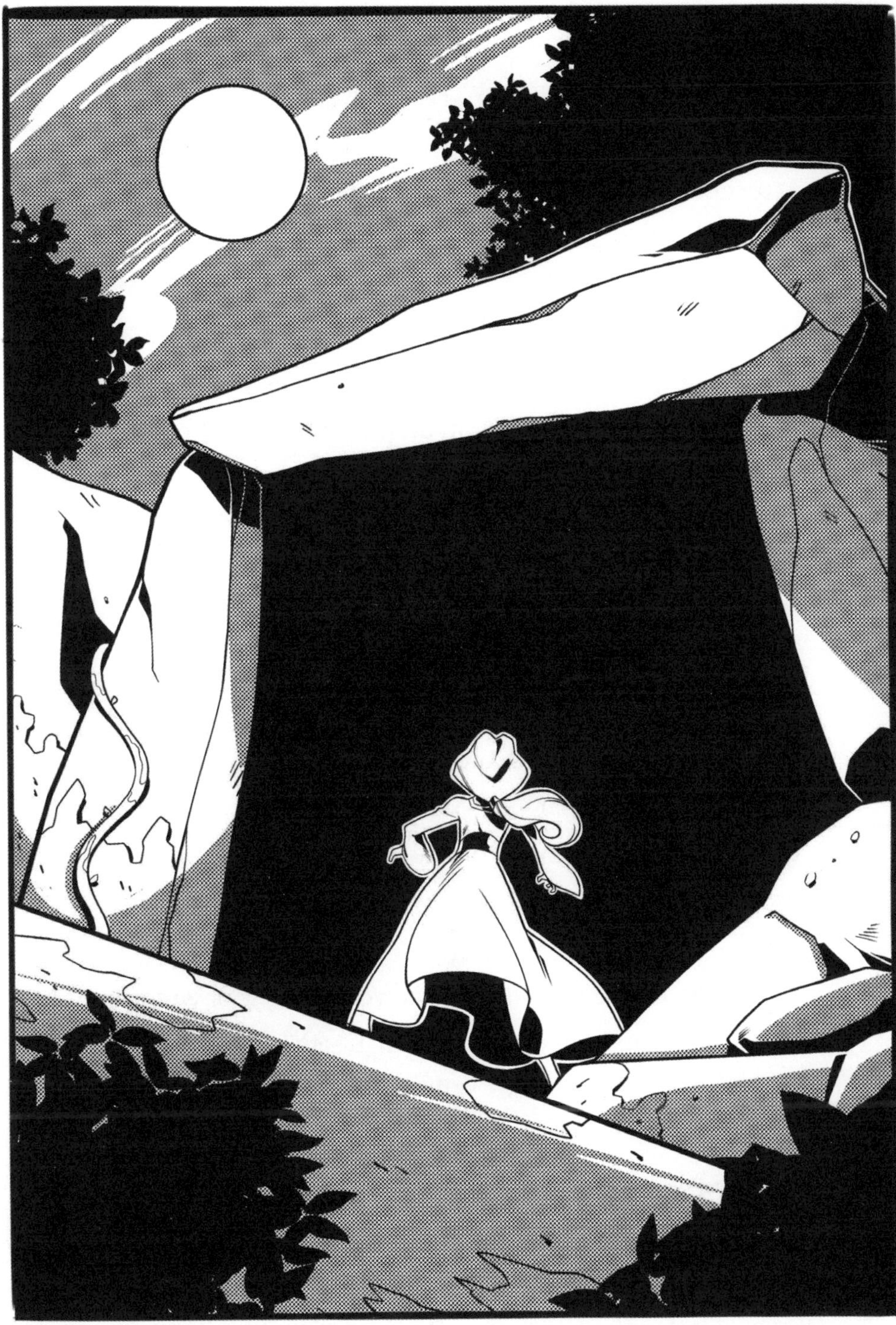

Decide & Survive: Agent 355

It's tricky to write an article that makes sense but also has code phrases in the correct places. It takes all afternoon, but you eventually create something that does the job well enough. You've always been good at writing, after all. When she wasn't off being a spy, your mom read you *Aesop's Fables*, *The Arabian Nights*, and poems from *The Spectator* magazine. Had things gone differently, you might've become a poet or playwright.

On your way to the newspaper office, a trio of British soldiers in the street seem to be staring at you. It's so hard not to run or flinch at every sound. Their eyes on your back make your skin prickle.

Carefully, slowly, you walk like a normal person doing normal things. No one hollers "STOP!" as you enter the newspaper office. No one levels an accusing finger at you as you pay for the ad to run in tomorrow's issue with money you "borrowed" from Aunt Myrtle's handbag.

Whew. It's been a while since you've done spy work. Good thing you haven't lost your touch!

General Washington will soon know about the British reinforcements and their plan to take on the French, thanks to you.

➡ **TURN TO PAGE 31.**

It's hard to hear anything with all the laughter, eating, and clinking of mugs. But over the hubbub of Major André's Christmas party, you catch him saying three things.

West Point.

£20,000.

British commission.

Aunt Myrtle never trusted Peggy Shippen. Sure, she loves the British, which your aunt admires, but she seems to love power and money even more.

And her husband, Benedict Arnold? He's as proud as he is annoyed with American politics. The idea of him helping the British capture West Point—a key military base in New York—doesn't seem at all farfetched.

It's EXACTLY the sort of sneakery Major André would be involved with, too.

What now, Agent 355?

⮕ **TO ASSUME THE WORST ABOUT THE WEST POINT PLAN AND DIRECTLY CONFRONT BENEDICT ARNOLD, GO TO PAGE 62.**

⮕ **TO ALERT THE CULPER RING THAT BENEDICT ARNOLD MIGHT BE PLANNING TO SWITCH LOYALTIES, GO TO PAGE 96.**

The soldier's breath smells oniony when you get close. But you have a job to do, and you worry that if you leave the document under a rock, by the well, or inside a rotten stump, it might not be noticed quickly enough. If your fake military document goes undiscovered, it's worthless to the Culper Ring and the Patriot cause.

"May I help you, ma'am?" he grumbles.

"Indeed. A pair of scruffy men—Colonials, no doubt—were brawling outside an inn just up the road. Thankfully, some of the King's men ran them off." You wince at pretending to be one of those Loyalists who support the tyrant, King George III. "This fell from one of their pockets."

The soldier reads the note, then squints at you. Is he suspicious?

"Why didn't you deliver this to the soldiers?"

"They went after those chuffy rebels," you say. "I recalled that soldiers were working here so I came directly."

He grunts. For a moment, you think he doesn't believe you. Should you run? Stay? Your heart hammers away in your chest in a mixture of fear and excitement.

Before you can decide, he bows. "You've done your king a service here, lady."

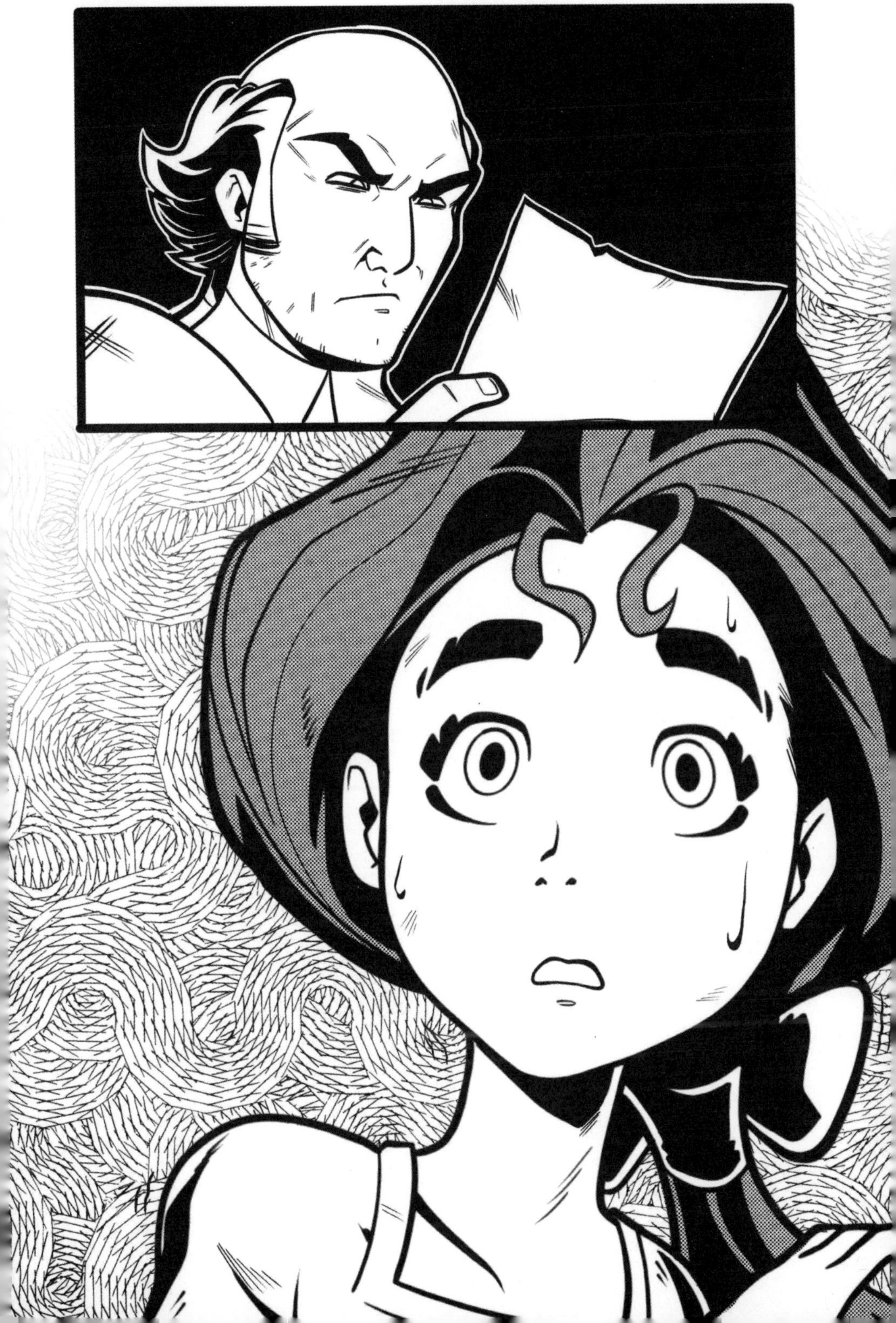

"My pleasure."

That was a close call!

➲ **TURN TO PAGE 69.**

Everyone at the party is in high spirits, and the evening is filled with loud laughter and joyful conversations. The food is extravagant—roasted quail, buttered walnut biscuits, and turtledove pie. The drinks are just as plentiful, with a variety of imported wines and ales from the British Isles.

In one corner of the room, a group of musicians plays traditional melodies on the fiddle, mandolin, and guitar. The guests clap along and sing, enjoying the festive atmosphere. At the center of the room, a large cake is set up, decorated with the rectangular red, white, and blue banner of the Union Jack—the British flag.

"Have some cake!" Aunt Myrtle says to you when the cake is finally cut. You have a taste, but it's too sweet. It's impossible not to think about Ethan starving away on a prison barge.

As the night goes on, some of the guests break out their muskets and pistols and begin to fire into the air in celebration. This is followed by a grand parade of people marching in formation around the house, singing "Rule, Britannia!" and "The King Shall Rejoice."

While you regret not following through on your promise to help defeat the British, there's no point

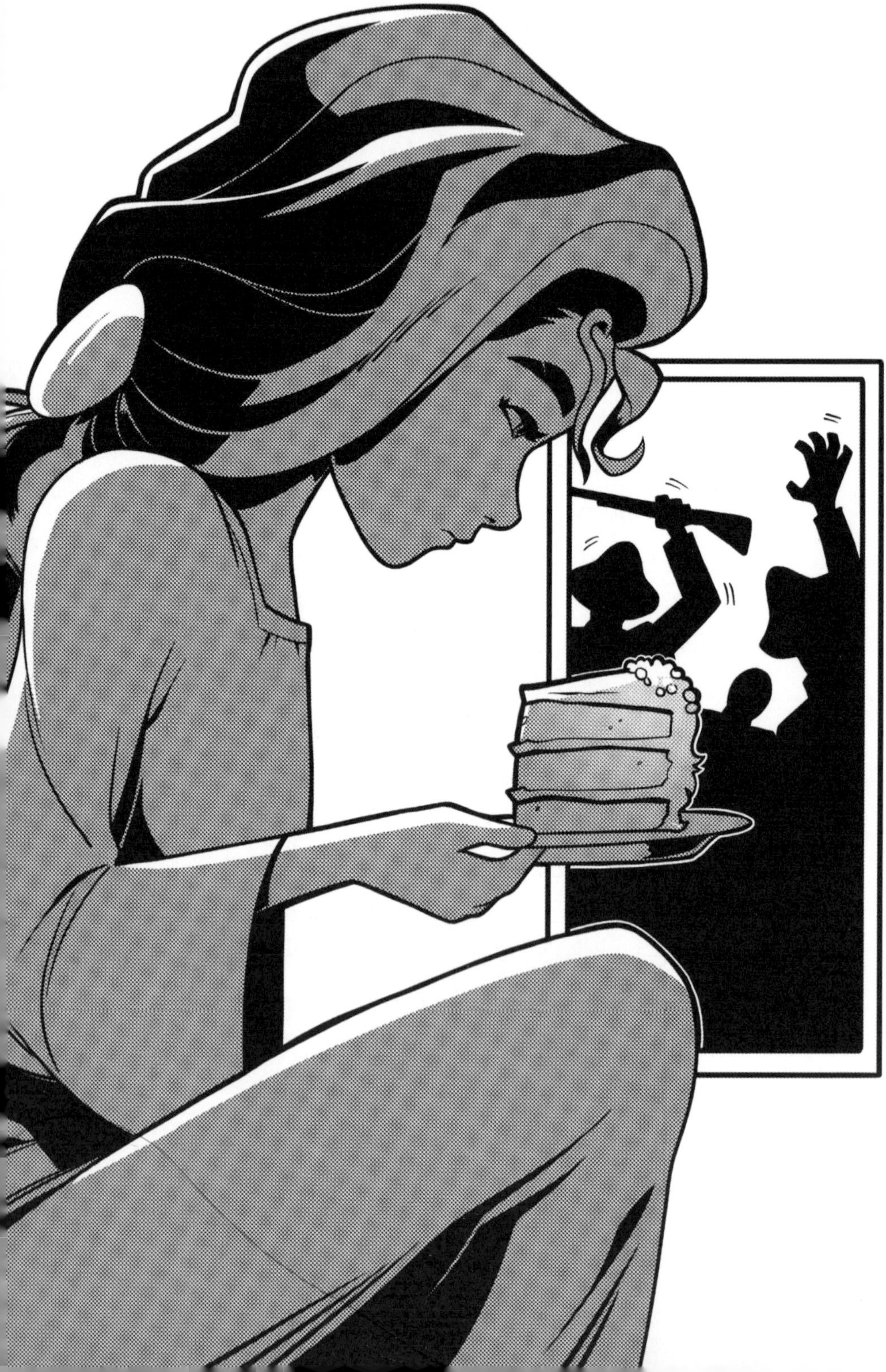

trying to be someone you aren't. You're just a kid, after all. What can you do to change the course of history?

THE END

**THE TRUE EVENTS
BEHIND AGENT
355**

THE BACKDROP: THE AMERICAN REVOLUTION

The American Revolution—when the thirteen colonies fought for their independence from Britain—was a pivotal time in American history. While many of the people and events in these pages are based in reality, there's a bit of imagination and creativity at play, too, to make *Agent 355* an exciting interactive story.

Here's a timeline of events surrounding the American Revolution that are firmly based in history.

1763 | PROCLAMATION OF 1763: *King George III issues the Proclamation of 1763, which forbids colonists from settling west of the Appalachian Mountains.*

1764 | SUGAR ACT: *Britain enforces the Sugar Act, taxing molasses and sugar imported by the colonies, causing tension between Britain and the colonists.*

1765 | STAMP ACT: *Britain passes the Stamp Act, which imposes a tax on printed materials in the colonies, leading to widespread protests and boycotts.*

1767 | TOWNSHEND ACTS: *Britain enacts the Townshend Acts, which impose taxes on goods like glass, paint, and tea imported by the colonies.*

1770 | BOSTON MASSACRE: *Tensions escalate between colonists* and British soldiers in Boston, Massachusetts, resulting in the deaths of five colonists during a confrontation.

1773 | BOSTON TEA PARTY: Angered by the Tea Act (which the British Parliament passed on May 10, 1773—the Boston Tea Party was in December of that year), a group of colonists, dressed as Mohawk Indians, dump 342 chests of tea into Boston Harbor in protest.

1774 | INTOLERABLE ACTS: The British Parliament punishes the American colonies for the Boston Tea Party with a series of oppressive laws.

1774 | FIRST CONTINENTAL CONGRESS: In response to the Intolerable Acts, representatives from twelve of the thirteen colonies meet in Philadelphia, Pennsylvania, to discuss their grievances and plan a course of action.

1775 | BATTLES OF LEXINGTON AND CONCORD: The first military engagements of the American Revolution occur as British soldiers confront colonial militia in Lexington and Concord, Massachusetts.

1775 | SECOND CONTINENTAL CONGRESS: Delegates from all thirteen colonies meet in Philadelphia to coordinate their resistance against British rule and establish the Continental Army.

1776 | DECLARATION OF INDEPENDENCE: The Second Continental Congress adopts the Declaration of Independence on July 4, announcing the colonies' separation from Britain.

1777 | BATTLE OF SARATOGA: The Continental Army, led by General Horatio Gates, defeats the British at the Battle of Saratoga, New York, marking a turning point in the war.

1777-1778 | WINTER AT VALLEY FORGE: The Continental Army, led by George Washington, endures a harsh winter at Valley Forge, Pennsylvania, testing their resilience and commitment to the cause.

1778 | TREATY OF ALLIANCE WITH FRANCE: France formally recognizes the United States and enters the war against Britain, providing crucial support to the Continental Army.

1780 | BATTLE OF CAMDEN: The British Army, led by General Charles Cornwallis, defeats the Continental Army at the Battle of Camden, South Carolina, in a major setback for the American forces.

1781 | BATTLE OF COWPENS: The Continental Army, led by General Daniel Morgan, scores a crucial victory against the British at the Battle of Cowpens in South Carolina.

1781 | BATTLE OF GUILFORD COURTHOUSE: The British defeat the Continental Army at the Battle of Guilford Courthouse in North Carolina. Although the British technically win, they suffer significant casualties and loss of momentum.

1781 | BATTLE OF YORKTOWN: General George Washington's forces, with French support, force the surrender of British General Cornwallis at Yorktown, Virginia, effectively ending the war.

1783 | TREATY OF PARIS: The Treaty of Paris is signed in France on September 3, officially ending the American Revolution and recognizing the independence of the United States.

Ryan G. Van Cleave

SPYING IN THE REVOLUTIONARY WAR: A BRIEF TIMELINE

APRIL 19, 1775: *Revolutionary War starts*

JUNE 1776: *Assassination attempt on George Washington.*

SUMMER 1776: *George Washington forms a secret committee to start gathering intelligence.*

AUGUST 1776: *British forces occupy New York City.*

SEPTEMBER 1776: *Nathan Hale is hanged for spying against the British.*

1777: *America is flooded with counterfeit paper money.*

NOVEMBER 1778: *Culper Ring is formed.*

AUGUST 21, 1780: *Benedict Arnold tries to take over West Point.*

JULY 1780: *Culper Ring stops attack on French navy.*

OCTOBER 9, 1781: *Revolutionary War ends.*

NOVEMBER 25, 1783: *British evacuate New York City.*

MEMBERS OF THE CULPER RING

The name "Culper" was created by George Washington, who fondly remembered Culpeper County, Virginia, his childhood home. While this impressive spy network had numerous informants, helpers, and sympathizers—such as New York City tailor Henry Mulligan and Long Islander Anna Strong—the following people were the primary members.

- **ROBERT TOWNSEND ("SAMUEL CULPER, JR."):** *a quiet Quaker merchant and newspaper reporter from Oyster Bay*

- **AUSTIN ROE ("724"):** *a Setauket tavern keeper who brought messages back and forth from New York City under the excuse of buying supplies for his tavern*

- **CALEB BREWSTER ("725"):** *an ex-whaler and lieutenant in Washington's army who ferried messages between Connecticut and New York*

- **ABRAHAM WOODHULL ("SAMUEL CULPER, SR."):** *a Long Island farmer and son of a prominent judge*

- **JAMES RIVINGTON ("726"):** *the owner of a fancy New York City coffeehouse and print shop, where he regularly overheard British officers gossip about military matters (including secret ones)*

- **AGENT 355 ("LADY"):** *the mysterious spy and the star of this book!*

The head of the Culper Ring, Lieutenant Colonel Benjamin Tallmadge, only knew one or two of the spies' actual names. George Washington didn't know a single name! That's how important secrecy was to this group.

WHY DO PEOPLE BELIEVE AGENT 355 EXISTED?

The main evidence that supports the existence of Agent 355 is a single letter from Culper member Abraham Woodhull to George Washington in 1778. He wrote: "I intend to visit 727 [New York] before long and think by the assistance of a 355 [lady] of my acquaintance, shall be able to outwit them all."

In an October 1780 letter, Woodhull wrote that "several friends" have been captured by the British, including "one who hath been ever serviceable to this correspondence." Woodhull was so upset by this situation that he uncharacteristically stole a lot of money.

Was it to bribe prison guards to release these prisoners?

Was it because—as some believe—he was in love with Agent 355/Lady and he'd do anything to save her from dying aboard a prison ship?

Decide & Survive: Agent 355

What do you think? Are you persuaded that Agent 355 actually existed?

WHO *WAS* AGENT 355?

Historians still don't know Agent 355's identity, but they've made several guesses over the years. Here are some of the leading candidates.

MARY WOODHULL UNDERHILL
Sister of Abraham Woodhull, she ran the boarding house in New York City where Abraham often stayed.

BETTY FLOYD
Cousin of Robert Townsend, her father was a signer of the Declaration of Independence.

ANNA SMITH STRONG
She relayed signals to a courier who ran military and smuggling missions for George Washington.

PEGGY SHIPPEN ARNOLD

Wife of traitor Benedict Arnold, she might have hidden secret messages in personal letters.

ELIZABETH BURGIN

A war widow, she regularly brought food to prisoners on ships and helped over 200 of them escape.

SARAH HORTON TOWNSEND

Sister of Robert Townsend, she was courted by a British army general.

THE CULPER CODE BOOK

To keep their messages secret, the Culper members often used invisible ink. They also created a code book consisting of 733 numbers that represented specific words.

If their messages had to use actual numbers (such as the exact amount of approaching British troops), they had a system to replace numbers with letters.

If they needed to use a word that wasn't included in the 733 words within the code book, they had a system for that, too.

Here's how a typical Culper spy message looked:

It is better to offer no excuse than a bad one.
—George Washington

284 283 60 634 436 413 169 vbep 1 feh qpi —711

("than," "bad," and "one" don't appear in the Culper Code Book, so they would be written out in the letter substitution.)

To the right, you can see a page from a real Culper Code Book. Only four books were ever produced. If you look carefully, you can see how certain numbers corresponded with specific words.

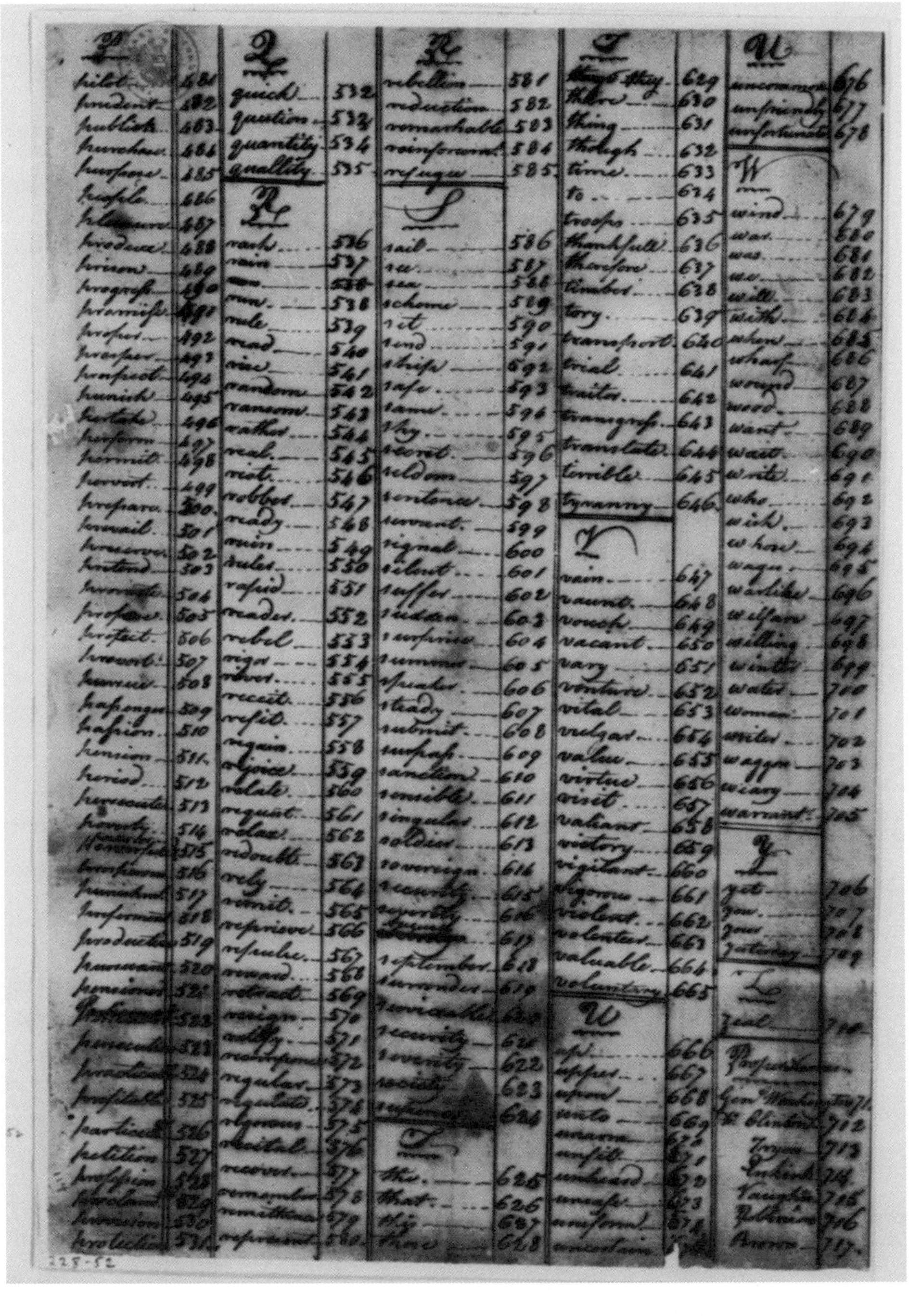

THE LIVES OF WOMEN IN THE AMERICAN REVOLUTION

At the time of the Revolutionary War, women were expected to be at home taking care of farms and families. Though it was mostly their husbands and sons who went to war, women at the time cared fiercely about independence, and many chose to fight for it.

Women joined in revolutionary riots and refused to consume English goods. They'd even attack merchants who refused to boycott prohibited English goods. Others fought with words, such as Phillis Wheatley, a Boston slave whose patriotic poems became popular in America and abroad. And there was Mary Katherine Goddard, who took over her brother's newspaper and published the first copy of the Declaration of Independence in it to inspire Americans.

To help the war effort, women became "camp followers" who cooked food, emptied chamber pots, herded cattle, foraged for food, cleaned hospital wards, and fed and bathed patients. Others worked as maids, laundresses, water bearers, and seamstresses. Women quickly became so indispensable that they received pay. Most got two dollars a day at the start of the war, but by the end of it, many earned up to eight dollars a day.

Though women weren't allowed to serve in the army or the militia, women such as Deborah Plimpton disguised themselves as men and fought. Plimpton—who went under the name Sam Gay—reached the rank of corporal before she was found out and imprisoned.

More women helped in other ways, too, such as New York teen Sibyl Ludington, who rode twice as far as Paul Revere in a massive rainstorm in April 1777 to rouse militia forces in New York and Connecticut against the approaching British soldiers.

Woman from all backgrounds recognized the value of America's independence, and they stepped up to help as best they could.

SELECT BIBLIOGRAPHY

ARTICLES

DeWan, George. "The Mystery of Agent 355: Unraveling the case of the Patriot spy who never was." https://www.newsday.com/long-island/history/the-mystery-of-agent-355-unraveling-the-case-of-the-patriot-spy-who-never-was-1.7512149

Elhassan, Khalid. "10 Significant Things About the Culper Ring, George Washington's Most Important Spy Network." https://historycollection.com/10-significant-things-about-the-culper-ring-george-washingtons-most-important-spy-network/8/

History.com editors. "The Culper Spy Ring." https://www.history.com/topics/american-revolution/culper-spy-ring

Messina, Juliana. "Spying for George Washington: The Culper Ring." https://www.saturdayeveningpost.com/2019/07/spying-for-george-washington-the-culper-ring/

Schellhammer, Michael. "Abraham Woodhull: The Spy Named Samuel Culper." https://allthingsliberty.com/2014/05/abraham-woodhull-the-spy-named-samuel-culper/

Seven, John. "Why Did Benedict Arnold Betray America?" https://www.history.com/news/why-did-benedict-arnold-betray-america

BOOKS

Allen, Thomas. *George Washington, Spymaster: How the Americans Outspied the British and Won the Revolutionary War*. New York: National Geographic Kids, 2007.

Captivating History. *The Culper Ring: A Captivating Guide to George Washington's Spy Ring and its Impact on the American Revolution*. CreateSpace, 2018.

Foner, Eric. *The Story of American Freedom*. New York: W. W. Norton, 1999.

Kilmeade, Brian and Don Yaeger. *George Washington's Secret Six: The Spy Ring that Saved the American Revolution*. New York: Sentinel, 2016.

Rose, Alexander. *Washington's Spies: The Story of America's First Spy Ring*. New York: Bantam, 207.

PODCASTS

"Agent 355." *History Nerds*, March 4, 2020. https://anchor.fm/brielle-brosier7/episodes/Agent-355-eb8o3k

"Morton Pennypacker: Long Island Spy Hunter." *The Long Island History Project*, episode 46, 2017. http://www.longislandhistoryproject.org/morton-pennypacker-long-island-spy-hunter/

"Scott Wolter." *The Malliard Report*, April 10, 2018. https://www.malliard.com/scott-wolter-3/

VIDEOS/FILMS

"Brad Meltzer's Decoded: The President's Secret Inner Circle."
https://www.youtube.com/watch?v=W4yLzC85w3Y&ab_channel=HISTORY

"George Washington's Long Island Spy Ring."
https://www.youtube.com/watch?v=Rq9VwhU_RV8&ab_channel=IntlSpyMuseum

"How a Secret Spy Ring Influenced the Birth of the US."
https://www.youtube.com/watch?v=VF8fg58tW68&ab_channel=BBCReel

WEBSITES

www.theculperringspies.weebly.com/mapsrouting.html
www.blackrockhistory.org/
www.history.com/news/george-washington-general-espionage-culper-spy-ring
www.womenhistoryblog.com/2011/12/agent-355.html
www.intelligence.gov/evolution-of-espionage/revolutionary-war/culper-spy-ring
www.britannica.com/topic/Culper-Spy-Ring

ABOUT THE CREATORS

DR. RYAN G. VAN CLEAVE is the author of dozens of fiction, nonfiction, and poetry books for both children and adults. When Ryan's not writing, he's crisscrossing the country, teaching writing at schools throughout the United States. He also moonlights as The Picture Book Whisperer™, helping celebrities write stories for kids and bring them to life on the page, stage, and screen.

MIKE ANDERSON is a comic book artist, illustrator, and animator. A proud husband, father, and year-long Halloweener, Mike loves pizza to an indecent degree. Some of his clients include Scholastic, Subway, and Walmart, among others.

MILK & COOKIES is the middle-grade imprint of Bushel & Peck Books, a children's publisher with a special mission. Through our Book-for-Book Promise™, we donate one book to kids in need for every book we sell. Our beautiful books are given to kids through schools, libraries, local neighborhoods, shelters, and nonprofits, and also to many selfless organizations that are working hard to make a difference. So thank you for purchasing this book! Because of you, another book will make its way into the hands of a child who needs it most. Do you know a school, a library, or an organization that could use some free books for their kids? We'd love to help! Please fill out the nomination form on our website, and we'll do everything we can to make something happen.